DUNCAN JEFFERSON

I0592845

THE
MISSING

Cover by Jenn Reece at
WWW.TIGERBRIGHTSTUDIOS.COM
Interior design and typesetting by Write Dream Repeat
Book Design
WWW.WDRBOOKDESIGN.COM

9 8 7 6 5 4 3 2 1

Paperback ISBN:

Dom's
STORY

THE ICY WATERS probed deep into his body, numbing his vitals and freezing his will to live. A ravenous wind howled across the lake under low grey skies, spitting spray into his face. Great clouds raced down the mountainsides, only to be driven back at the last moment by unseen forces emanating from the violently churning waters of the lake.

Only a few moments ago, the small ship's sail had been cutting like a dagger through the wind with great speed. Now the sail lay like a deadweight, sticking to the surface and refusing all attempts from Dom to raise it up with his only hand. Blood oozed from the stump of his right arm where he'd tried to secure a rope, leaving his good hand free to do the work of two. The blood mixed with the waves and seemed to feed the fury all around him.

He clung to the hull of the small upturned vessel and screamed at the bundle of rags fast drifting away from him. That bundle was the ferryman who'd promised that the storm was just a passing fancy and that the passage would be swift and easy. Dom had heard the hollow crack as the smashed mast struck the ferryman's head in that terrible moment when he himself was thrown into the wintry waters of Lake Como.

Although the shore was only a few hundred yards away, the wicked wind lifted the waves against him. It taunted him as it blew great chunks of foam into his face and matted his hair over his eyes. His clothes felt like leaden weights welded to his body. He lay on his back and tried valiantly to thrash his way like an upturned turtle towards the tantalizing shoreline, but it was all in vain. He sank. His lungs threatened to burst, and he was on the cusp of relaxing into the final swoon of oblivion when a strong hand grabbed him by the scruff of the neck and pulled him up to the surface

"I've caught a fine one here, lads," sounded a voice in his ears.

Dom was pulled into a boat by unseen arms and slumped into its wet wooden bosom like a newborn babe. His screaming lungs devoured the rain-filled air, and for a moment his mind delighted in the fact that he was still alive. Then the shivering began. The powerful wind, in addition to the chill caused by his wet clothes, drew out what heat remained in him, and he shivered uncontrollably.

"Wrap that around you before you freeze to death," the rough voice repeated, as its owner pushed an oilskin blanket over him. "No point taking a dead 'un ashore with us, is there?" And whilst his voice was rough, his hands carefully covered Dom with an oiled shell that kept the wind from its prey and life in his body.

Perhaps the wind lost interest in the small boat once its fingers could no longer claw at the heart almost in its grip. Or perhaps the storm was just passing, but the winds eased and the rain lessened, and the little boat made it safely to shore. Dom was not able to move his frozen limbs, and he had to be lifted from the water sloshing in the bottom of the little boat and carried ashore like a baby. Callused hands began to rub life back into his arms and legs, and slowly he was able to rise to his feet with the aid of his rescuers and stagger toward the shelter high above the water line.

The door of the building slammed behind them as they entered, caught by a final venomous gust of wind. Dom slumped down on the floor near the only source of heat, a small fire pit in the center of the room. He stayed there transfixed by the flames, which threw off eddies of heat that warmed his body. Slowly he began to test more of his muscles, whilst behind him came the sound of other people taking off wet clothes and dropping sodden boots onto the wooden floors.

"Where am I?" he asked, still looking at the fire.

"You're alive, and that's all you need to know at the moment," came the reply from behind him. "Here, eat this. It'll put some life in your arms and legs." Dom turned and put out his only hand to receive a piece of bread, which he transferred to his mouth before accepting a mug of something steaming hot. He cuddled the mug next to his chest with his stump, whilst his hand ripped the hard crust in his mouth.

"What happened to the other one?" said the stranger, nodding towards Dom's stump.

"Nerves," replied Dom. "My mother always told me not to bite my nails," he said, with a weak attempt at humor. He tore off another piece of bread, dipped it in the soup, and ate it as if it were the best food that had ever passed his lips. After a few minutes, he paused his eating and said to the fire, "I've never been so cold in all my life." Then turning once more to the man who'd saved him, he added, "I never thought I'd feel warm again. Thanks for pulling me out. I'm in your debt."

The man who'd saved him, and who'd warmed and fed him, now came around and stood in front of him. The man was wrapped in a thick wool blanket, and his feet were shod in thick sheepskin boots. His bearded face gave little away. He was probably in his late twenties, but looked much older. There was a gleam in his eye, which was difficult to understand: it was either madness, which made Dom very nervous, or else it was inspired—and that carried its own problems.

"Did your mother warn you about peeping through keyholes, too?" the man said, pointing his crust of bread towards the cicatrized socket that had once contained Dom's eye. Dom's hand involuntarily went to his face, and he blushed at the ugliness that he knew the other man saw.

"Must 'ave come off in the water," he mumbled and returned his gaze to the all-seeing fire.

"You're a queer one, and that's a fact. Here you are, sitting in front of a warm fire with a full belly and breathing God's pure air—present smoke excepted—and you're worrying that we don't find you pretty enough." His glittering eyes danced playfully in the firelight. "I don't suppose it would take too much skill to knock another patch up, would it, eh? I'll ask around and see if we have a dressmaker with us who can do a little needlework."

With that, Dom's rescuer drained his mug and headed off to join his companions, who were seated on wooden stools around a wooden table. Half-spent candles barely lit the gloom, revealing a crusty loaf and a steaming iron pot. The man sat at the head of the table, then spoke again out of the gloom. "When you're ready, there's some blankets in the corner, and you can bed down and rest until you get your strength back. Later on we'll get the cook to make us something special, and after that you can tell us who you are, where you came from, and most importantly, where on earth you thought you were going on such a dreadful day. Don't bother to dress up, you'll find us all very informal here." He spoke between sips of soup, and every word he said was laced with a delicious humor and greeted with a rumble of laughter from those in his company.

Whether it was the heat or having a warm meal in his stomach or just the shock of being so recently on the cusp of death, Dom was soon overcome with tiredness, and one yawn chased another. He crawled into the corner and within seconds was fast asleep. How long he slept was a mystery, because the dark winter light within the hut was the same when he woke up as it had been when he went to sleep.

"How long was I asleep?" he asked the pair of eyes that watched him as he rose from the blankets, wrapping one around himself to retain the blessed lingering warmth.

"Does it really matter? Food's not ready yet, it's dark outside, and it's still raining. Sleep seems like a real good option if you ask me," a voice replied, but a kindly voice at that.

Dom wandered over to the table and slumped down. His arms ached, his legs ached, and his neck felt like he'd slept in the back of a stone quarry cart for three days.

"Here," said the man, "see if that fits," tossing something across the table to him. Dom picked it up and smiled. It was an eye patch with fine needlework around its perimeter and a black ribbon to tie behind his head.

"I'm much obliged," he said quietly. "My little nieces in Rome will be delighted that they have such a well-dressed uncle when they see me again." And tying it on, although such a simple act with such a tiny piece of material, he felt fully dressed once more.

"What's that delicious smell?" he then asked. "He wasn't joking when he said the cook would prepare something special, was he?" And a happy, contented smile appeared on his face.

His savior and host appeared and announced that supper was almost ready. Several forms took shape from the black piles littered around the fire pit and came to seat themselves around the wooden table.

"We'll eat first, and then we can listen to our friend's story with the comfort of full stomachs, dry socks, and a warm fire," he added. He put a large pewter platter with three cooked fowl and two large rabbits down in the middle of the table. He then went to another room and returned with two jugs of steaming liquid and four big crusty loaves. One of his companions passed around the platters and mugs. Then the men bowed their heads whilst their leader said a prayer of thanksgiving and a blessing on them all.

Dom was amazed. He looked up and down the table in the orange light of the wax lamps and saw four men leaning in to take their food and hungrily eat it, be-smirching their beards and whiskers with the fatty, yet delicious food. He thanked his neighbor for pouring the steaming, aromatic red liquid into his mug and took a sip. The first one burnt his lips, but its herbal aroma and cinnamon taste lingered on. As it cooled and he re-joiced at the pleasure of eating such an unexpected feast in such an unexpected place, the alcohol in the mulled wine reached his brain, and he eased into the company of those around him.

There wasn't much talk—they were all too hungry. This was the first time they'd feasted like this for some days, and they were wary, too. A stranger can be a blessing or a threat, and only after they'd heard his story and made their judgments would they loosen their tongues, too.

Plates and platter were scrubbed clean with the last crumbs of the crust, and fingers were dipped deep into mugs to wipe out the very last of the mulled wine. The men pushed their chairs back and looked to the head of the table, where their leader and cook sat watching them. "Come," he said, "let's build up the fire and hear how the one-armed man came to be looking for his lost eye in Lake Como on a wild and wintry day." He paused and looked at Dom, saying "The floor is yours, brother, you have our full attention."

Dom bowed his head in acknowledgment and began to stand up before speaking, as was the custom. "Stay where you are," his host called out, "your standing will be measured by your words and not by your physical disposition." Sitting down again, Dom began his story.

"My name is Dominic Acciai. I was reared by my grandfather Poppa, who was a forester from Abruzzo. He worked for a merchant in the city of L'Aquila and cut wood and hunted wild boar for him when he could. My sister and I were sent to our Poppa at a very early age. He was a widower by then: a good, kind, and wise man, and still very strong despite his years. He'd head out into the forest each day to find fallen timber, and depending on its size, would bring it back to the house. If it was a full-grown tree, then he'd harness his horse to it and drag it back through the forest. He'd then spend the next few days cutting it into lengths for timbers, saving the leftover bits for the winter fires. I can still smell those pine trees and feel the sticky resin from the twigs that we swept up and used as kindling. And I remember how at night the wood would crackle and spit in the fires, and the dried pine needles softened the floor we slept upon.

"Of my parents, I knew very little. My father had been injured in a small skirmish amongst the warring factions that were always with us in those times in Abruzzo. He just grew old too soon and slowly faded from life. He'd sit in a corner with dulled eyes, watching the embers and hardly speaking a word to anyone. My mother was a beauty, so I'm told, and many suitors came to seek her hand in marriage when our father died. But she'd loved him too much to take another. Perhaps that was why she loved and protected us even more. I can't remember her face anymore, but her smell and the feel of her arms holding me close to her bosom are still as real as they ever were. My sister, who was older than me, said Mamma had lovely smiling eyes. She said Mamma tried to hide her sadness when she was with us." Dom paused for a moment as if trying to see his mother in the flames that danced lightly in the fire before them. The group waited in respectful silence for him to continue.

"She rejected the suitors, but then wicked rumors began to spread that she was a witch who shunned the company of men, and even that she'd been the cause of her husband's death. But I knew nothing of all this. My sister Ann told me that in the dead of night, things were left outside of our house—terrible things—and then no one came to visit us anymore. Mamma arranged for us to secretly leave and go to our grandfather some way distant from L'Aquila." Dom sighed a deep, wounded sigh before going on. "After we had gone, a crowd of people came up the road one night with flaming torches and dragged her from the house. They beat her and poured tar on her. Then they took her outside of town and threw her on a big fire. In seconds, the tar took light, and she was burned alive as a witch. They killed my gentle, loving mother in such a violent, hateful way." And looking around at the others, he said, "Why do people do such wicked things? There's nothing brave about burning a weak and frightened woman. Why do these monsters hide their own fears behind such terrible deeds?"

"Of course, we knew nothing of all this until a long time later. Perhaps Poppa knew, but the dear man kept it to himself. From the moment we arrived, he never ceased to love us as his own children for the rest of his life.

"Those were hard times, but good times, too. We lived and worked as one, with Ann caring for the house and for her 'men' as she called us, whilst Poppa and I worked together in the forest. When I was small, I used to lead the horse and make sure it had enough feed for each day. As I grew and became stronger, I joined him with the axe and the double-handled saw. We all thought that I would take over from him someday because I was such a big, strong lad. But the fates had other plans.

"Poppa was getting old, and the plague was always visiting our area. One day we came home from the town to find him close to death. He smiled his beautiful smile and thanked us for bringing so much joy to the later part of his life. But as he said, God was calling him to a new country, and he'd have to leave us behind for now and go and join his wife and daughter. That simple thought made our tears so much easier to bear. He died soon after, and we buried his precious body deep in the forest under the trees he loved so much." Dom pulled on his earlobe, remembering each detail as if it had happened just yesterday. Then with a deep sigh, he continued, "And so the two of us were left alone once more—or at least we thought we were."

"I'd never really thought about Ann being good-looking, but Poppa said she looked so much like our Mamma. When I think back, she was a really beautiful young woman. But it was that beauty that betrayed her.

"The local duke had a bastard son who made his intentions known to her in the most dishonorable ways. But she rejected him every time. Even as Dom remembered all of this, a fire crackled in his eyes, and his fist clenched tight on the table. "Bastard by heritage and bastard by nature. He was an evil man as well as a persistent one. One afternoon, I came home early. I'd broken the axe handle and needed to get another when I heard her screams coming from the house. That bastard son was attempting to ravish her and had beaten her several times around the head to try and subdue her. I dragged him off her and hit him as hard as I've ever hit anything in my life. He fell, hitting his head against the ground. I can still hear the crack of bone on rock—it's a sound you never forget—but I was wild with rage, and the dog deserved it.

"I knew straight away that we were in serious trouble. There was a man lying dead in our house, and his father was the duke. I knew it wouldn't be long before the news reached the palazzo, and then he'd have us hunted down and killed without a moment of regret. We had only one thing on our side—time. We hoped beyond hope that the son had told no one where he was going, so we dumped his body in the river and trusted to the good Lord that it would be washed miles downstream before it was discovered. But we were wrong. It got caught in a fallen tree only a mile down the river, and his friends soon worked out where he'd been.

"But Ann and I must have been blessed by the gods. That very evening we fled with only the clothes on our backs and took the road to the north—Ann on our horse and me on foot. After a few miles, she stopped and got down. She looked at me and said that if one of us was to survive, then we must part ways. If God were to doubly bless us, then we might both survive. But in our hearts, we knew that the men who followed us would be vicious in their vengeance and that our slight hope of survival was to try to divide their group. I chose the wild road through the forest, and she took the main road with the horse. I chose a hidden life, and she chose the open way that hopefully led to an aunt in a convent in Siena." Dom stopped and stared at his clenched fist which he now relaxed. "I've never seen nor heard of my sister since." A mug of mulled wine appeared next to him and looking up, Dom saw the face of a compassionate man. "Thanks, friend," he said and carried on with his story.

"Being a woodsman, it wasn't hard to survive, but life on the road for a young man isn't easy—especially in winter. I'd trap animals for food and fur, and work for a wage when I could.

"One day I met another man on the road who simply wished me a good day and smiled at me. His name was Gino. He saw that I was hungry, so he shared the little bit of food that he had. The two of us sat whilst our stomachs savored every small morsel that went down into them. Gino had an easy way with him, and when he got up to go, I went with him. It was as simple as that. It wasn't until later that I learned of his early life and how similar it was to mine. Looking back, it's funny to think that the one thing we had in common was suffering, and it brought us together. His Papa was a simple man who was as honest as the days were long. But being honest can lead you into some terrible places, too, and it led to his Papa's murder. Do you know what those murderers did to him after they'd butchered him? They cut out his tongue and nailed it to the wall of his shepherd's hut, just to show how brave and powerful they were. Gino thought about hunting them down and killing them, but on the inside he was stronger than they were. He stayed true to himself and true to the memory of his father.

"We became like brothers, traveling the roads, working when we could, and having fun when we could, too. But Gino deserved better than a lonely life tramping the roads. One glorious day he found his childhood sweetheart, who'd never stopped loving him. It was as if he'd suddenly become complete when they first set eyes on each other after so many years.

"He stayed on with her and her old father. I cried when we parted. Mainly they were tears of happiness, but they were tears for me, too.

"Just before that happened, we'd met up with Rosso, another of our lost generation. The three of us had some great times together before Gino stayed on with his sweetheart.

"Rosso stood out in any crowd, mainly because of his red hair and white skin, but he was an angry young man on the inside. That anger threatened to consume the good and kind heart that he tried to keep hidden. But like most of us at that age, he was as green as grass. Gino took it on himself to guide Rosso into the wider world, which was a good thing because at that time, as Rosso himself admitted, he could have gone either way.

"It was around this time that we met Villeprieux. He was so different from the rest of us, which perhaps is why he seemed attractive to us. Where we were dowdy young men living a life in the shadows, he was French, good-looking, well traveled, and educated. But looking back now, he was more lost than we were. I'll admit that he had a way with him, and after Gino left, he took over as our leader. That was probably the worst mistake we ever made. Soon we found ourselves as mercenaries in a fight we had no business being in and for a cause we knew nothing about. Villeprieux showed us some gold and told us of the great bounty we would get when the battle was over. He didn't tell us that he'd sold us out to the other side, or that if we got caught, that we'd be killed or tortured.

"I was supposed to be his bodyguard. He told me to stay with him at all times, probably because I was the biggest person there. He didn't tell me that as soon as the fight began, he would turn his horse and run, leaving the rest of us to fight his war. He showed his true colors then. He was a traitor. He'd been passing information onto the enemy. He told them to overpower me first, and once they'd done that, the rest of us would surrender. But the enemy didn't do that. Instead they slaughtered our men. They dragged me behind a horse around the camp and then laid me down by a fire. They teased me about how big I was and what a great view it must be 'up there where your head is.' Then they said, 'Well, let's see how good the view is through one eye,' and taking a branding iron from the fire, they put out my eye. I screamed like a baby, which seemed to make them laugh even more. Then their leader appeared and asked what was happening. When they told him I was Villeprieux's bodyguard, he smiled and said, 'I don't think he'll be needing your services anymore,' and with that, he cut off my sword hand and left. They all thought this hilarious and left me."

Around Dom, the room fell silent. Outside, the icy wand of winter had transformed the rain to snowflakes. Yet in that silence, even they could be heard softly tapping against the window panes.

"I don't know how I got to Rome, and I didn't know where I was, even when I got there. Some urchins found me in a doorway, and . . ." Here the Dom paused, "and then he appeared out of nowhere." Tears appeared in the big man's face and streamed down his face as his body shook with silent grief.

Wiping the salt away from his face with his sleeve, he cleared his throat and took up the story again.

"I'd been in my own mad world for so long. But then I felt a pressure on my chest, and when I opened my eye everything seemed clearer. I'd been dreaming that Rosso was telling me stories, and one of them had made me smile. When I awoke and saw a ceiling above my head and four cozy walls around me, it felt like a new dawn. I looked down to see what was pressing on my chest, and I saw his head." And smiling broadly at the memory of it all, he went on, "at least I saw a bald head surrounded by a flaming ring of red hair. I knew the familiar smell of his body and immediately I knew it to be Rosso, even though that shining, bald pate confused me for some minutes. Then a stranger with a kindly face appeared at the door. He smiled with a look that told me he knew it was Rosso, too, and he was happy to see the two of us back together in the land of the living. It turned out this man was called Pietro. 'I'm just an ordinary man,' he'd say—but I'd say that's the last thing he is. Pietro is one of the most extraordinary men I've ever met."

"He cared for me, which was a real challenge. You know, it's a funny thing, when you are healing from a great hurt, every day you look at the same world as everyone else, except that you look at that world through a lens crippled by physical and mental scar tissue. The only way you can know that you're getting better is by looking back and seeing how far you've progressed. Healthy, normal people never have to worry about that. They go forward each day expecting life to be good and hoping that happy things will happen to them. It was only a very long time after, when I felt truly normal again, that I realized that the terrible wounds I'd suffered would never leave me. The magical thing was, though, that whilst I was recovering, they had somehow changed. Instead of being the heavy burdens that ground me down each and every day, cutting me off from people and the ability to really enjoy life, they'd now become my companions. Now, instead of carrying those wounds, they walked with me. And not only that, they'd become a key which allowed me to unlock wounded doors in the lives of others who'd suffered like me. These badges of shared suffering have allowed me to enter gently and quietly into their lonely place—without any sort of judgment. I like to think that I'm a sign to them that their life has hope and a future, too."

Dom had stopped talking. He'd drifted into a remote part of his mind and was unaware that he had been talking to himself. He'd forgotten that he was in a room with anyone else, but they'd all understood what he had said. And the words that he spoke were like the undoing of small and big locks in each of their minds, letting light into the dark places and darker thoughts they'd all hidden during their short lives.

Dom looked up and smiled at his companions, "Apologies, friends, my mind still wanders. Some things never change, eh?" And with a wry grin, he picked up a leg bone that was on the plate in front of him and waved it at the group as he continued his story.

"Sharing a meal," he said, picking a missed morsel from the white bone, "that's a special time, too. Being alone can lead you into some bad habits, but when you share a meal with others, then your body and mind are fed at the same time. Up until that time, all I'd thought about was getting my strength back and getting accustomed to the ugliness that I saw in my reflection: an ugliness I felt guilty about, although none of it was my fault in any way. Although I was getting stronger, I was scared to meet other people. I was living like a recluse in Pietro's room and becoming my own worst and most critical companion."

"Then they sprang what they called their conspiracy." Dom chuckled quietly to himself. "I thought we were just going for a walk in the gloom of the evening, and I'd hoped that the shadows would hide my deformities and my scars. We went down a darkening alleyway and into a dingy doorway, but nothing prepared me for what was on the other side. Children."

"It was a taverna really, but it was also the home of a big family who were friends of Rosso's. Little children tumbled out of the rooms and into the eating area. They hugged Rosso and his friend, the monk Julian, who was their uncle. Then they turned and hugged me, too. I was totally unprepared for those innocent arms that threw themselves around my neck and told me they loved me— and me a stranger with one eye missing and a useless stump of an arm. There is something so utterly cleansing about being climbed over by a two-year-old who pulls up your eyepatch and says, 'what happened to your eye,' then hops off again before you get a chance to answer because he has seen something more exciting, like food or a cat walking into the room. It made me realize that although that eye may have meant the world to me, the world was still a wonderful place with many other wonderful things to see and do. All I needed to do was to see it with the eyes of a child.

"Watching a child eat is a pretty liberating thing, too, for a man with one hand and one eye. Although I might be slow to eat, and sometimes I drop food on the table, I'm no longer so self-conscious about it all. Whenever I stumble like that now, I think about watching one of their little ones eat. He was eating his pasta with such a studied concentration, and yet there was a wasteland of dropped food all around the plate and on the floor. His face was smeared with sauce and drink, yet the looks of delight from his proud parents were enough to warm the saddest man's heart.

"They eventually gave me a home and with it came a new hope. Living with that family linked me back to life through the many experiences shared with those little children. They weren't the only ones to thrive in the love showered on them by their parents and friends. I was restored to life, too.

"The parents made room for me in their home, and I helped out in the kitchen in return. But the children found a place for me in their hearts, and as they grew and learned, I grew and learned, too.

The sound of benches scuffing the floor as stilled limbs were stretched suggested it was time to take a break. "That is a strange story, Dom, and I suspect that there's still much more to hear, but perhaps we'll wait till tomorrow to hear more of that. My name is Niccolo, and my patient friends are called Francesco, Carlo, and Cristofero." Here the three companions stood and greeted Dom with open arms, kissing him on both cheeks like a welcome friend. "We are traders," said Niccolo. Francesco, Carlo and Cristofero all looked at each other and smiled. "But we have an unusual trade. We trade in good deeds," he said and held his arms out with palms upturned. "And you know what, we haven't made any money yet. But then again, we think we're very wealthy men," and he came down and gave Dom a big hug and two kisses, too. "But now it is time to rest again, and perhaps in the morning you will tell us more of what brought you to this part of the world, and at such a risk to your own life. So sleep and heal, my friend, tomorrow is another day, and it comes full of hope for us all."

The night was long and cold, but Dom slept deeply and woke refreshed. He washed his face with cold water and stirred the embers of the fire into life before joining Niccolo outside to watch the mists roll down the towering mountains that walled in the waters of the lake. Last night's snowflakes had warmed to rain.

"It's beautiful, isn't it?" his host said. "Even though it's winter, and it's raining, and everything you see is grey, there is something wonderful about it all. Unless you've got aching limbs, of course, and then it's pure murder." He gave Dom a nudge, and they both laughed freely. "Come on, let's rouse the others and break our fast, there's more of your story to be heard, and I suspect that you might be pressed for time, if I'm any judge of human flesh." And reentering the shelter, they prepared food for the whole group, then woke them to fill their stomachs.

"Rosso was studying at Santa Maria Maggiore and had decided to enter the Augustinians," said Dom, once their stomachs had been satisfied and empty platters pushed back. "He never did convince me that he actually knew why he had made that decision, but as he still hadn't taken his final vows, I think he always thought he could back out at the last minute if he had to. Anyway, being an orphan like so many of us, one thing that he really cared about was the abandoned children he met around Rome. Whenever he came across any of them, he always did his best to feed them, clothe them, and if possible find homes for them. He had some successes, but it was very hard because there were just so many of these children.

"One of the ones he'd found was a little girl called Clare. He'd seen her one day in the market square where she'd been abandoned. It was her great fortune that she met Rosso, because he found a home for her with the local smithy, Marco. He and his wife Laura are wonderful people, and they have their own little family of three children—two boys and a very capable older sister called Sarah."

"Well, one day—out of the blue—Rosso was commissioned by Cardinal Visconti to deliver a message to another Cardinal in Paris. They told him it was because he could speak French so fluently, and they couldn't trust any of the usual couriers, there being so many spies in the Vatican. Well, Rosso decided to take Clare with him because there was a chance they might find her real parents in Paris.

"He never did tell us what the message was or much about what happened whilst he was away. But when he got back, Clare was still with him, and she went back to living with Marco and his little family. Later on, he told us that they'd discovered who her father was, but he was dead. And as for her mother, he told us that there was no lead whatsoever." Dom paused and gave a wry chuckle, "If you knew Rosso, then you'd know he's a very bad liar. We all knew that he must be hiding something. It was Brother Julian who found out. It turned out that Ville-prieux was Clare's real father, though how that came to be, we still don't know. But what we did know was that Rosso hadn't told Clare the whole story yet. Julian also found out that Rosso had been warned never to inquire who Clare's mother was, for both of their sakes, which was a bit of a mystery and a worry to us all.

"Anyway, everything seemed to settle back into a regular routine. Life with my new family at the taverna meant everything to me. And Rosso returned to his studies, whilst all the time trying to avoid any thought about the looming day of his final vows.

"And then he disappeared.

"Brother Julian came running into the tavern early one morning, which caused great alarm because Julian never runs anywhere, and getting up early in the morning is not his strongest habit. He kept repeating 'Rosso's gone—he's just disappeared!' and it took us several minutes to get him settled and try to work out what had happened." Dom paused as if trying to reorient himself after waking suddenly from a deep sleep.

Then having found his mental landmarks, he continued, "I need to backtrack a few years. It was just after the battle when we became separated." Just the mere mention of those evil times inscribed their horrors onto his face. His hand involuntarily went to the empty eye socket, and he pulled his wounded arm back as if it were about to be severed once again. The sudden stillness in the room was total, as all felt the terror of Dom's horrific memories.

"Rosso had been found by a woman who'd dragged him from the field of slaughter, floated him away upstream to safety, and nursed him slowly back to health. She was the one who had taught him his words, and how to read, too. I think he loved her, but he'd never experienced that sort of love. The closest he'd ever come to experiencing any sort of love was with his little sister Anna, and she'd died all too young. Perhaps it was this memory of innocent love that had him referring to the woman who took care of him after the battle as his much-loved sister Agnes.

"She told him that she'd had smallpox when she first arrived near Siena, and the disease had left her face badly marked. But it always made us smile to see that big redheaded monk with his tonsured dome, dressed in a black robe, telling us about his Agnes's brown eyes and her beautiful, wavy hair. I think the only one who didn't realize that he loved her was Rosso himself. They used to write to each other when they heard of someone going in the other's direction, and when a letter did arrive from her, he'd rush off to a quiet spot and devour every word. His face would be alive with happiness for hours afterwards. He was so proud of her and her wise words." And looking up at his comrades, Dom added, "Sometimes we men just don't see what's in front of our faces."

"Rosso said that Agnes was kind to everyone and would always help the most vulnerable. Recently she'd been helping another young man who had stumbled into her path. He wasn't a soldier or suffering any obvious illness, but he wasn't quite right in the head, which was how Rosso put it. Apparently, he was well educated and could both read and write. In fact he'd told her that he'd once been a scribe to a learned man in Milan but he'd been cheated out of his wages and badly beaten for his reward. Perhaps that's why he had the falling sickness, which made him foam at the mouth and bite his tongue. Who knows?

"But back to the story. When Julian had settled down enough to tell us his story, we went to the monastery on some pretext to pick up a bundle for Clare, and we searched Rosso's cell. It didn't take long. Monks don't have much in those cells of theirs. But we did find a letter from Agnes, torn and crumpled in the corner. When we'd pieced it all back together, we had a bit of a mystery. In the letter, she'd written that she hoped it found him well, but she wouldn't be writing to him again as she'd decided to marry this man Stephano and go and live in his region—but she gave no clue as to where that was. She wished Rosso well in the rest of his life, but begged him not to try and find her as she'd made her mind up, and it would be pointless for him to even write to her.

"Rosso's mind must have exploded like a volcano when he read those lines. His foundation stone had just been blown up under his feet. That was when he up and left. Brother Julian talked with the novice master, Brother Bart, who's a kindly man, and who seemed to know Rosso's mind better than Rosso did himself. He told Julian that Rosso had recently been reading the works of an Englishman called William Flete, an Augustinian like himself, who'd come to the Siena area to live a simple life in a cave. People had started to call him the Brother of the Woods. By all accounts, he's a very holy man. They say he knows our own Catherine from Siena, and he's heard her confession, too." This final piece of information made all those present look at each other, and an eager look infused their eyes. Everyone had heard of the famous Catherine.

"Go on, brother Dom," said Niccolo.

"Well, according to Brother Bart, the writings of Brother William had deeply affected Rosso, and it was the novice master's humble opinion that was where Rosso would be headed—to the caves near Siena. So after we'd left the monastery, we went to the taverna that belongs to our friend Gian. We also sent messages to Laura and Marco, and to Pietro, to let them know the news of Rosso's sudden disappearance.

"The three of us came to the conclusion that the letter from Agnes had been the tipping point. Why else would he up and go to live like a hermit with this English holy man? Why else would he turn his back on the world—a world where there was no more Agnes and no more love? But after some deliberation and some good common sense from Gian's wife who said, 'Just let the lad be,' we decided to do nothing for the time being and wait for Rosso to contact us.

"Oddly enough, we didn't think it strange when we didn't hear back from Pietro immediately. Perhaps that was because it's in his nature to just disappear for days or weeks at a time. Sometimes he'd be absent because he was in so much pain with his back that he literally couldn't move. At other times it was because he was doing what Pietro always does, helping those less fortunate than himself, whoever and wherever they are. But we did find it odd that we'd heard nothing back from Marco or Laura. So after a couple of days, I decided to pay them a visit.

"When I got to the forge, it was shut up tighter than the timbers on a ship. No one seemed to be certain where they were. Some said they'd heard that Marco had been called to the country to visit a sick father, whilst others said that Laura had been called away to family somewhere near Naples—but no one was really sure. I went back to the Taverna and told Gian what I knew, and we came to the conclusion that all we could do was wait.

"A couple of weeks later, Pietro appeared, looking older and leaner than usual. He was exhausted, and his back was obviously causing him great distress, although he never uttered one word of complaint. He declined the seat offered to him by Gian's wife, but gladly accepted food and wine. When he'd finished his meal, he ran his fingers through his hair and said 'Kidnapped!' That was the only word he uttered: 'Kidnapped!'

Pietro's
STORY

AS YOU KNOW, I live a quiet life. I have my room, and from its one door I can stand and watch the dance of humanity as people go about their affairs, living the life of normal souls.

It would surprise you to know how much I see that people don't think I see. Just because I walk slowly with a cane doesn't make me blind or deaf, but it does seem to make me invisible to a lot of people who prefer to rush and bustle through life.

I like to think that I notice the little things. But when you add them all up, they can sometimes create big things. I find that each little thing has its own beauty, like the way seedlings can appear halfway up a fortress wall. Or how spiders' webs can be strung with dewy beads between towering trees, and how secret lovers will dart lovers' looks and smile as only lovers can. I also see little people who've been discarded by bigger people and left to fend for themselves in a cruel world. I like to think that I can help them, and they seem to respond to such kindnesses. It's these little people who are even more invisible than I am, and yet who hear things that sometimes they shouldn't really be hearing. These little ones are closest to my heart. I am honored when they confide their secret confidences in me, even if they haven't a clue what any of it may mean.

It was one of these urchins who just happened to mention that he'd seen some strangers down at the market a few weeks back. He said just that: they were strangers and that they acted 'different' to the rest of the stall-holders and customers who roamed randomly around the piazza. "It wasn't that they was dressed different," he said, "it's jus' that they smelt different. Must 'ave been scent or summink" was his conclusion. It didn't register with me at the time, so I put it aside in the recesses of my memory. Then a few nights later, I was woken from my sleep by knocking on my door. It was that lad again, but this time he kept saying, "There's summink funny goin' on at Marco's place. You'd better come quick and see this," and having given his message, he disappeared into the darkness.

I can't rush things, but I dressed as quickly as my body allowed, grabbed my cane, put my beads in my pocket, and set out for the forge. The sound of my stick tapping along the cobbled streets sounded like stones being thrown down from a great height. Everywhere was dark and silent. Thankfully the moon was halfway through its cycle, and the night was clear. I avoided all the detritus left behind from the day before, and after a time, the open area that was the piazza fanned out in front of me. The silence was palpable. The gentle music that's rarely heard from the fountain's flow echoed off the walls and shuttered windows of the surrounding buildings.

The small figure of my urchin friend appeared out of the fountain's shadow and came towards me. "Over 'ere," he said and led me to the forge. The windows were barred and shut. The forge doors had been sealed with a heavy chain and fastened with a large padlock. The place was silent and empty.

"I 'eard 'em earlier," he said, wiping his face with his sleeve as he ate an apple I'd brought with me. "They 'ad Marco trussed up like a chicken, but 'e was still givin' 'em a real ta-do. It took four of 'em to bundle 'im into the cart, then they all piled in on top of 'im and gave 'im a real wot-for. Then out comes the muvver with a rag stuffed in 'er mouf, kicking and struggling like a wild cat. I reckon she did more damage than poor ole Marco. And then four blokes wiv four bundles flung over their shoulders appears—I reckon that was the kids, but they couldn't do nuffing. Then, quick as a flash, they was gone. They must 'ave muffled the wheels of that cart, 'cos it 'ardly made any noise whatsoever." And swallowing the last piece of apple core, he wiped his face once more.

"Did you see any faces or recognize any of them, laddie?" I asked him.

"Give us a chance, Pietro," he objected. "It's bleeding dark out here at this time of night, and I ain't no bleeding owl. But I'll tell you this, remember those blokes I told you about the uvver day? Well, I couldn't see much, but they smelt the same. Sort of scenty—nuffing like you and me, if you knows what I mean."

"Do you know which direction they're heading in, then?" I asked my satisfied spy. He smiled broadly, and the light of the moon was reflected in his teeth.

"I may be a kid, Pietro, but it don't mean I'm stupid. There's about 'alf a dozen uvvers like me what sleeps in small places near 'ere. You'd never spot them unless you knew where to look. Like human dormice they is, tucked up all warm and snug in some dry drain, or behind a rain barrel. As soon as that there cart 'ad turned the corner, I upped and woke a couple of 'em and give 'em orders to follow that cart, and not ta stop until their little legs was fallin' off. So I reckon I should be getting some news when the sun comes up. But those little blighters is goin' to be mighty 'ungry when they gets back," he said, looking up at me with big pleading eyes.

"Don't you worry, they shall have their stomachs filled until they cry for mercy," I replied, with a smile to match his. Then putting my hand on his shoulder, I slowly turned to head back to my room.

"I'd better wait 'ere, Pietro. It's me what they'll be looking for, and I'd better wait for 'em. Don't you go worrying about me, you get off 'ome and get some rest. After all, a man of your age shouldn't aught ta be out on a cold night like tonight." And with that he gave a wink and disappeared into the gloom. It's an oft-stated fact that the bravest hearts can often be found in the most unlikely of people. If that's true, then that little urchin was to be counted amongst the elite of them.

I walked back to my room in those dark hours before dawn and thought how totally alone I seemed to be in such a busy city. And yet a hidden thread tied me to so many unseen souls, and each of those threads was so vital to the integrity of the woven garment that is my life.

I don't have much in my room, just those things that I find essential: my chair, my bed, and a small desk beneath the window where I can sit and read or just sit and watch. Food is not a big part of my life, but I knew that those small children could eat their weight in bread and meat given half a chance, especially after the night they'd had-- which meant that they'd have an extra layer of hunger to deal with. So as soon as the marketplace began to stir, I was down there buying what I could to help fill and reward their willing bodies, and listening for any gossip that might be abroad.

I needn't have hurried so in my purchases, because it wasn't until nearly noon that three tired and hungry ragamuffins appeared in the street and headed for my room. The poor things were bone tired, almost too tired to eat, but at the smell of the fresh bread, their hearts lifted and their mouths opened. And soon there was the usual pushing and shoving that is an intrinsic part of children's play.

"Is there any more, mista'?" a little girl called Lola asked, wiping the last crumb from her platter.

"I'm so sorry, Lola," I replied, "you've just eaten more food than I normally eat in a week." But I was very happy that they'd eaten so much, even though there was nothing left to give them.

"That's OK, mista'. That was more than wot I've ate in the last mumf." And she gave me a huge smile of thanks. "'ave you 'ad enuf, Coppino?" she asked the little lad, who turned out to be her brother. His mouth was still so full, all he could do was nod in the affirmative. "You should 'ave seen little Coppino last night, mista'," she continued, looking up at me with pride. "'E might appear a little small, but them little legs of 'is can gallop as fast as an 'orse when 'e gives 'is mind to it. 'E followed that cart all the way to the big 'ouse up at Monte Sacro, dodging in and out of doorways whenever they slowed down to see if anyone was following. Little Coppino 'ere could 'ide under a leaf, I reckon, and no one would notice." She gave the little man a big hug, smacked a kiss on his forehead and rubbed it in "so that the fairies can see 'e's a precious little man."

Their leader, who'd stayed out all night waiting for them, was known to his small flock as the Bishop, and he now took charge of the small gathering. Tucking his thumbs into his jacket, he said, "If I was one of them proper bishops, then I fancy that I'd make youse both Cardinals." And bowing low, he addressed his companions: "Your Heminences Cardinal Lola of the Pantheon stables and the most majestic Cardinal Coppino of the Colosseum's caves."

"Well, if we is Cardinals, then that means you should kiss my hand," said Lola, holding out her fingertips for him to kiss. And we all laughed happily at the innocent fun of it all.

"I've heard of sillier suggestions than yours, Bishop. And come to think of it, some of the new Cardinals aren't that much older than you are, and they probably aren't half as smart as you, either," I said. "But back to your story, did you get any news as to where they've taken Marco and his family, or did you get any clue as to who kidnapped them?"

"Dunno," piped up little Coppino. "They took 'em to that convent up at Monte Sacro and then the cart 'eaded off back to the city. I 'ad to fink what was the best fing to do. So I upped and followed the cart, 'cos I thought to miself that the convent weren't going to go nowhere in the meantime. Trouble is, Monte Sacro's a long way from 'ere, and it's just as far comin' back, too," he added, with the innocence of logic. "And even I get tired after a bit of a gallop. So I was mighty pleased when them blokes stopped at a place to get some vittles. For miself, I got some stuff from a nice lady wot serves there. But then she give me a clip round the ear and told me to 'be off' 'cos her master was watchin.' When them blokes came back out ta the cart, I just up and said, 'mind if a young lad gets a lift inter town, Signori?' and the bloke what was in charge just shrugged his shoulders and said "'op on then, laddie,' and off we goes right up to the Vatican itself. I slipped off before anyone of 'em seed me, but they just 'eaded straight fru the gates, and that was the last I saw of 'em."

The news that the little boy uttered sent a cold shiver of fear through me. Although the Holy Father may speak of peace and love, he seems to surround himself with people who would kill you before you could tell him what your problem is. And why would he have such a dangerous interest in a smithy and his little family? I faced a real dilemma: I couldn't walk into the Vatican and ask to see the pope and then demand he tell me what he'd done with my friends. Knowing some of the superiors of the religious orders around this blessed city, I was certain that asking them for information would be met with a silence more deafening than the grave itself! The mere thought of coming between a Reverend Mother and her Holy Father sent an uncontrollable shudder through me.

I looked at the three dirty faces that had finished their eating and were smiling back at me.

"Got a problem, Pietro?" asked the Bishop.

"I'm afraid this is a little out of my league," I answered honestly. "I don't have the resources to spy on the pope and his Reverend Mother up at Monte Sacro," I said, taking my beads out of my pocket and running them through my fingers like the old Arab had taught me. This had its usual calming influence and allowed my face to relax into a smile to match their own.

"I dunno, Pietro," said the Bishop, running his fingers through his manic hairstyle. "I fink you're losing your grip. Now if you 'ad the smarts like the free of us"— and here he put his arms over the shoulders of his two mighty companions—"you'd know that 'idden behind us is 'undreds of uvvers like us. Not even the 'oly Farver or 'is most Reverend Muvver ever stops to fink about we little scavengers wot lives in rubbish 'eaps or in cold doorways on a winter's night. Now it's my belief, Pietro,"— by now the Bishop had stood up, and grasping his tattered jacket by its soiled lapels, had begun to walk around the small room in a most professorial sort of way—"that if you was to send us free out to talk to certain members of our invisible family, then I fink that we'd find 'em fairly willin' an' more than able to watch wot these people is doing and where they is all a goin' to. You'd be amazed at 'ow many of us little 'uns does this every day of their little lives. Just give 'em a chance, Pietro, and they'll see fings you'd never notice and get the information youse wants as soon as it 'appens." Then looking at me archly, he added "and most of 'em owes me anyway." And planting his feet wide apart, he puffed out his small chest and dared me to deny him.

Although my face ached with a smile at his simple conviction and unplumbed courage, what he was suggesting was to pit street urchin brains and brawn against some of the most cunning and often vicious adults in the whole of Italy.

"Do you have any idea of what you're asking me to let you do, Bishop? Are you sure you want to place Lola and Coppino in a situation that could be seriously dangerous?" I pleaded with him. A sadness descended on his face and he seemed to shrink just a tiny fraction.

"'Ave you any idea of wot it's like to live like we does, Pietro? Every bleedin' day we face a beatin' or a baitin'. 'nd little Lola 'ere 'as to deal wiv stuff that'd make you tear yer 'air out wiv rage. It ain't a bowl of roses out there, you know. You is one of the few what acherly stops to see us, and it's 'cos you've been so good to us urchins that we want to 'elp you." He looked at his little friends, who both nodded their heads in agreement. "We ain't putting ourselves inta danger, we is just puttin' ourselves inta a different danger. We ain't stupid, we don't want to get hurt or killed, but if we can 'elp someun as who's 'elped us, then we is up for it, ain't we?" And again he looked at his two tiny champions, and they nodded their wise heads once more.

I had tears in my eyes as I walked around the small table to give them each a big embrace. "I don't think I've ever met greater hearts in all the adults I've ever met," I told them. "OK. Do what you think is best, Bishop. I'll wait here to hear back from you. Just be more careful than usual, you're not just dealing with villains and thugs now. It seems to me that there's something very dark going on here. So please, be very careful."

"You're talkin' to a pro 'ere, Pietro. Me an' mi crew is up for it. Leave it to the Bishop and 'is little flock, an' we'll shine our light into sum dark places, eh?" He grinned from ear to ear at his biblical parable.

I didn't hear anything for several days. But even I was beginning to get agitated and anxious when I hadn't heard from the Bishop for some weeks. During that time I become acutely aware of how many little children seemed to be roaming the streets, either on their own or in small groups. Some of them begged on corners, some sat in doorways simply staring at all the passersby, and some bore the marks of a recent beating. A pitiful few lay in disused spots, curled into little balls with vacant expressions on their faces. No one approached these littered lost. They were too far gone and would soon find rest and comfort in a pauper's grave. It broke my heart to have had my eyes opened to such terrible neglect, and yet see silken-robed, civilized people drive past in their scented seclusion.

When I met up with Brother Julian one day, he observed the extra agony that was plainly written on my face. "Having a bad day with your pains, Pietro?" he asked.

"Salve, Julian. No, it's not that. It's them, over there," I replied and pointed to a group of bedraggled, half-starved children who were playing knucklebones in the dirty street. A frown clouded his face, too.

"Ah, the terrible mystery of suffering," he said, and his round face softened into a troubled smile. "It's funny, you know, Pietro, how we put up with our own pains, but when we see the truly innocent suffer for no reason at all . . . ," and his voice trailed off into silence. But then he brightened and put his arm around my shoulder, adding, "But it's a challenge we've got to face, which means we've got to do our best without losing faith. It's my experience that we often feel pretty powerless in the face of so many who suffer so much. But if we look at it from another perspective, if we few who have become, how shall I say . . . enlightened: if we few affect a few others for the better, then I believe that they'll go on to affect others within their reach, and that little snowflake of hope will turn into an avalanche of love. So don't worry my friend, there are always going to be people of good faith, just like you, people who are a force for good. These people really want to make a difference, too, whatever anyone else might think about them." And as he finished off with an animated "Hallelujah" and a small jig of joy, we both stood and watched the unfolding scene in front of us.

"You've heard about Marco and his family," I said.

"Yes," he replied. "Strange business, that."

I hadn't seen Julian or his brother for some time and wondered whether I should tell them of my conspiracy.

"Are you off to your brother's place?" I asked my hummingly happy friend.

"As a matter of fact, I am. My niece is due to show me the fruits of her musical practice," he said with glowing pride. He added a quiet aside, "although I suspect that she's far more interested in what I have in my pocket," and with that, he patted a small bulge in the pocket of his soutane. "It's nothing, really," he added, with a broad smirk on his face, "just something to help tie back her hair."

"Would you mind if I came along with you, Julian? There's something I'd like to discuss with you all."

"That sounds mysterious," he said, "and there's nothing we monks like more than a really deep mystery. It comes with the job description." With that, he burst out into a wonderful "Gloria in excelsis Deo."

Julian's

STORY

STANDING IN THE choir stall always gives me a shiver of delight. I've been doing it for almost all of my thinking life, and yet each time I step up onto that wooden step to enter the stalls, I feel like I've entered a world of forgotten voices who in their own time were also awe-struck at that first step up.

And I love the wood with its glorious patina created by the soft brushing from so many different garments over so many years. Even the creaks from the planked floor seem to say, "Walk lightly. Because I, whom the world has forgotten, once stood here and sang praises to the Almighty One."

Then there are the candles, which in the silence before dawn sing their own guttural song and send sooty re-minders to the vaulted heights. But when the morning sun hits those stained windows, and their blackened stories spring to life with crimsoned saints and madonnas with clothes glowing with lapis lazuli, then music and song are the only ways to truly celebrate such wonders.

The good Lord blessed me with a sense of music and a voice that others appear to admire, and it gives me great joy to be able to sing and celebrate this wondrous life of ours. Most seem to think me a simple man who happens to have a gift for singing, but with song must come emotion, and I experience a great deal of life from my choir stalls in that great Cathedral. Even in the dark hours before dawn when we monks sing our Matins, I see those stooped widows creep like shadows behind the pillars of this great temple. I see them light a candle before a holy picture of Our Lady or some oft-neglected saint, and the yellow glow from the flame reveals their creased and tired faces. And I see them shuffle and slowly bend their painful knees and bow their heads in silent prayer. I often wonder what it is they say. Is it for themselves or for loved ones long gone? Or is it for forgiveness for hurts received and hurts dispensed? So often the dark light before dawn seems to consume them in silence, because when I look up from my music, the place where they knelt and prayed is vacant, with only a tiny flame to remind me of their presence.

And I see the drunks come in, boisterously noisy and staggering like mannequins whose strings have been cut. I watch as they cloyingly embrace a priest, telling him things he already knows about sins he is familiar with. Then he slumps into a safe slumber under the shelter of that ancient roof that has seen and heard so much. But most of all, I like to see the lovers come in. They truly understand what reverence is and what holiness means— it accompanies them in all their waking hours and they rejoice in the love they see reflected in the eyes they so delight in. Lovers really know how to smile: it's a smile that brings an ache to the cheeks and heightens every sense. It's the feeling I get when I sing something very beautiful that reflects the emotions that love brings to life in our hearts.

Although I love to sing, I also love to watch the world with all foibles and threats, with all its hopes and despairs. Yet even when everything seems bleak and dispiriting, I always find green shoots of hope, however deep the darkness of the moment. Perhaps that's why some think me simple, because I smile and sing, but they forget that I see and feel more than that. It's not my place to trouble the world with my own layer of dark thoughts, but that doesn't mean that I don't have them. I choose rather to transform them with my voice into something else, something that people can recognize and share: something that can shine a small light for a brief moment in their lives.

It's amazing how quickly the mind can move through all these thoughts, which is what I'd been doing on the morning when I met Pietro in the street. He seemed burdened by more worries than his normal one of constant pain—a pain he never discusses, but bears with great dignity. Pietro's a transformer, too. He turns his physical pain into a desire to help those who are even less fortunate than him. His little acts of kindness could fill a book and amaze all those who thought they knew him. But it is a book that will only be published at the end of time when we all get to see what we wrote in the book of our own lives.

Pietro and I greeted each other kindly, and he asked to come to Gian's with me as he had something he'd like to share with us. Seeing as it came in a conversation relating to the sudden disappearance of Marco and his family, my interest was immediately piqued. But as a monk I've learned to be patient, so we continued the journey to my brother's taverna, chatting about the little things we saw as we walked along. I was taken by the number of little urchins that he seemed to be acquainted with. "You've been taking lessons from Rosso by the look of it," I said.

"Any news from our tonsured redheaded novice, Julian?" he asked in return.

"Not a scratch of a quill have I or anyone heard," I replied. "He's searching for the meaning of life in a cave was what I heard. Alas, for someone of my shape and tastes, a cave is an improbable source of enlightenment, but you'd be surprised how many do see the light in such austere places."

When we arrived at the taverna, my little niece and all her siblings drove all thoughts of Rosso from my mind as they scampered around me, pulling at my robes and asking fourteen questions to the dozen. My little favorite slipped her hand in my pocket and pulled out the ribbon with total delight, then ran off to her mother to have it immediately put in her hair. That errand, once completed, was followed by her rushing back and hugging me and telling me that I was "the very specialest uncle in the whole wide world." In other words, it was a perfect start to a family get-together.

Gian came in, and we all embraced one another. Then most of the children left, and the three of us were joined by the Dom, who had one of the children on his shoulders—one who had a firm grip on his ears, too. Gian suggested in a fatherly way that the little boy "Put Dom down and go out back and play." The Dom let him down gently and smiled with ear-glowing pride as the young lad scurried out the back.

"Good to see you, Pietro. Are you keeping well? You look a little drawn; I thought the warmer weather would be good for your back," the gentle giant said.

"No, it's not my blessed companion," said Pietro, using a term he often used to describe the disability and pain caused by his back. "I've got some news and I'm not sure whether it's fair to share it with you," he said.

"Now you've really got my attention," said Gian.

"What's it about?" I asked. "You're not in any trouble, are you?"

Pietro fiddled with the empty glass that happened to be on the table. Then he sat back and pulled his beads from his pocket and began to run them through his fingers.

"It's not really about me, although what I have done could be seen as dangerous in some quarters, and it's that danger that I really don't want to inflict on anyone else. Especially someone who's got a young family." And here he looked at Gian, who in turn looked at me with confusion written on his face. After a pause where Pietro seemed to struggle with whether to say anything, he said, "Let me propose a situation to you. If your friend upset someone powerful in the Vatican, how far would you go to help them and would you involve anyone else in the situation?" The thought hung in the air like the threatening blade of Damocles that it was.

"I'd steer clear of that nest of vipers," said Gian in a most unchristian tone of voice. Then looking at me sideways, he added, "Present company excepted" and gave a theatrical wink whilst pouring me a glass of wine. "What do you think, brother?" he asked, when he was happy that we all had what we needed to make us comfortable.

"'Fools rush in where angels fear to tread' springs to mind. But then our little brother Francis was thought to have been the biggest fool of them all, and look what he's started" was my initial lighthearted response. But what Pietro was suggesting troubled me deeply. "Could you enlighten us a little more, dear Pietro?" I asked, hoping to get a clearer picture of what I already suspected.

Our friend looked at us one after another, took a deep breath, and then told us his story. Marco, Laura and their little family had been abducted in the night and nothing was known of their whereabouts. Pietro had found himself a small band of unlikely helpers in the shape of several urchins who roamed the streets unseen and unloved by the rest of the population of Rome. I knew some of these lads and lassies, and they did indeed have formidable minds in those wretchedly starved bodies of theirs. On the surface, they had little to lose in trying to help. But up against the powers of the Vatican? And against the religious order of nuns up at Monte Sacro? "What would happen if one of them is caught?" I asked Pietro. It was as if I'd punched him in the back, such was the expression on his poor face.

"I don't even dare to think about it," he said. "But I was powerless to stop them. Have you ever tried to get a child to change its mind when there's an adventure to be had?" And he raised his hands and eyes towards heaven as if to emphasize his powerlessness in the face of such a superior force. "So far there has been little to report. No one's left the convent according to my spies, but the Vatican is a different nut to crack," he said.

"Which convent are you talking about up at Monte Sacro?" I asked.

"It's the one at the top of the hill behind the Church there. My informants tell me there are more tunnels coming out from under it than there are rabbit holes in the woods nearby."

"I know that church well. I've sung there on many occasions—weddings, funerals, and feast days—so I know quite a few people. I'll see what I can find out from my friends there. But the Vatican, well, that's a totally different situation altogether. I think it's best to concentrate on where Marco and his lovely family were last seen and forget the men at headquarters for the time being," I said to my friends.

"As usual, brother, you have shined a bright light in a dark place, and I fully agree with you. For my part, I suggest we eat and drink some more. All this plotting and planning can weaken a man, and it looks like we'll be needing all our strength if we're to make any progress finding our friend the blacksmith and his little family." And rising to talk to his wife in the kitchen, Gian left us feeling a glimmer of hope.

"When I first came to Rome," Dom spoke softly to the two of us, "I was in a terrible way as you both know. I was a ragged mess, left to live in doorways where most people ignored me and only the very few dared approach to offer help." The memories ignited by his words flared briefly for a moment before he lifted his head and said with a half smile, "I think it might be time to relive those times down at St. Peter's Piazza. Just like your little urchins, Pietro, nobody sees or worries about destitute beggars, but they still see a great deal even if they've only got one eye." And the half smile on his face blossomed into a full one.

"Aren't we forgetting someone here?" asked Pietro. "What about Rosso? Shouldn't we be thinking about getting a message to him, wherever he is? After all, he and Clare were mixed up with that mysterious message from Cardinal Visconti to Cardinal Villeprieux in Paris, weren't they? I've a deep suspicion that the two events are linked in some way."

Gian returned with a jug of wine, some cheese and olives, and a loaf of fresh bread. "Just to get us started," he added with a broad smile. "Now, where were we?" he said, sitting down. He tore off a piece of bread and dipped it in the olive oil that was already on the table.

"I was just saying that we should try to get a message to Rosso, but we're not sure where he is," said Pietro. "And Dom here has suggested that he reacquaint himself with his former skills as a beggar, but this time go upmarket and ply his trade in St. Peter's Piazza."

"Wasn't it somewhere near Siena that the Englishman was living in a cave?" a now-thoughtful Gian offered. "That's not too far away from Rome, when you compare it with going to Milan or Sicily. And come to think of it, we have a farmer just outside of Siena who supplies us with the best olives in the whole of Italy. He's often asked me to go up there and visit him, but of course that's impossible for me with a business to run and a young family to care for." He paused to let the information sink in and then turned to Dom and said, "But if my partner was to take a trip to Siena and meet up with my farmer friend there, then he might get more news than he would sitting in St. Peter's Piazza getting a very numb backside." After a brief pause whilst the image of Dom rubbing life into his buttocks flashed through our minds, we all burst out laughing. Even Dom did, though his face was blushing.

"Thanks, Gian, for even suggesting that I am your partner. You know I would never let you down, but I think employee would be a better description, don't you?"

Gian, who was the eternal optimist amongst them and always seemed to find a smile, even when the others were enveloped in gloom, now adopted a more serious look. "Ever since you walked in that door, Dom, you've been my partner. It's me who's honored to call you 'partner.'" And then the sunshine returned to his face. He filled everyone's glass and then offered a toast: "To true partnerships." Glasses clinked, and we all took up the refrain. Gian's wife popped her head out of the kitchen and said, "Make sure you don't break any of those glasses. Pasta should be ready in 10 minutes." And then she disappeared again.

And so it was decided. I would head to Monte Sacro to see what I could discover there. Meanwhile Dom would head off to Siena to taste some olives, and hopefully find Rosso's trail and tell our redheaded mystic what had been happening in his absence.

My duties at Santa Maria Maggiore kept me occupied for some days, but I was able to send a message to a friend at Monte Sacro suggesting we collaborate on a music project together and that perhaps we should meet there to discuss my idea.

It was shortly after Trinity Sunday, when things tend to quiet down liturgically in the Roman Church—and which also meant that my singing services were in less demand—that I managed to slip away and head up to Monte Sacro. It's a lovely walk in the early summer if the sun is shining, but heavy, cold showers are just as likely. Unfortunately, it was one of those days, and even though the walk along Via Nomentana is a straight and easy one through the countryside, the rain and cold made it a miserable journey. I arrived at Monte Sacro with my clothes twice their normal weight with water, and twice as cold as when I started. And even though I describe myself as pleasantly rounded, that was not enough to stop my limbs from shivering from the cold.

"Come in, dear Brother," my friend whispered, with some degree of anxiety in his voice, "come sit near the fire and get some heat into your body. You must be frozen." As clouds of steam began to come from my drenched habit, he left me for a moment. Returning quickly, he said, "I've asked the cook to bring hot soup as soon as possible, but you shouldn't have set out in such terrible weather. Couldn't your travels have waited a few more days? There's no point dying from fever over a piece of music, is there?"

"I would have to disagree with you there, Brother," I replied through chattering teeth, "although I would prefer to leave this world feeling just a little bit warmer. I'm sure I'll feel better soon, and bless you for being so kind to me."

"The whole community here will rejoice with me once you've recovered from your journey, especially if you find you're able to sing with us at Vespers later on," he added, with genuine kindness in his voice.

"Thank you, Angelo," I answered. The trembling in my body slowly began to subside as the heat from the fire and the soup began to infiltrate my body.

The monastery at Monte Sacro was a small one, with only about a dozen brothers living there. They worked amongst the poor of the district, which meant that they were busy every day. The principal house was in Rome itself. For such a glorious city, Rome always managed to attract those who had fled destitution, only to find it again in the expanding metropolis.

Once I was feeling warmer, I was shown to the small guest room close by the kitchen. The room itself suggested that the brothers didn't intend for their guests to remain too long. It was simple and cold, with that musty dampness that leeches from the walls and into the lungs. It was close to the kitchen, which meant that the smells of cooking food were tempting—especially to someone like myself. However, the odors of past meals also lingered in the damp atmosphere, which had the reverse effect on one's appetite.

Looking back, I suspect that it was the combination of being soaked to the bone and the dampness inherent in the marshy air surrounding Monte Sacro that led to me coming down with a fever. My resulting illness had several consequences. First, I lost the ability to talk, as my voice was reduced to a whisper. You can imagine what a terrible trial that was to me. Then my appetite, already dulled by the stale smells in my small cell, waned, too. And you can imagine what an even greater shock THAT was to me! But as they say, every cloud has a silver lining, and the light within that celestial cloud came in the form of the apothecary, who was called from the nearby convent to prescribe some herbs, unguents, and inhalations for me, there being none in the small house where I was staying.

To my surprise, the apothecary was a nun, and a very wise and well-educated one at that. During her ministrations, she let slip that she was the fourth daughter of a minor noble in Marche who'd had no hope of bringing in a decent dowry, so had been sent to the convent in her late teens. But she was a bright girl and knew her herbs and tinctures. I was given medicines to take, ointments to rub on my chest, and a foul-smelling mixture to use as a steam inhalant. I'm not sure which of these worked, but over the next week, my voice slowly croaked back to life and my stomach renewed its love affair with food . . . and wine.

By this time, Sister Maria and I had become quite friendly, and she was delighted that my voice had returned to its former glory. "Perhaps, dear brother Julian," she said one day, "you might consider coming to the convent and singing a Gloria for our Sisters, in thanksgiving for having recovered from your illness!"

"Dear Sister Maria, you don't realize just how happy that invitation makes me," I answered with almost-guilty truth. "But won't you have to ask for permission from Mother before I can come?" I asked.

She blushed a little and said, "I took the liberty of suggesting the idea to her already, and she's given her permission."

"God is good," I said with a broad smile. I couldn't resist trying out my vocal cords on a simple hallelujah in praise and thanksgiving. "Do you often have guests at the convent?" I asked, as calmly as I could.

"Oh yes," she said. "Well, we did until recently, and then Mother told us 'No visitors and no visits unless I give permission'—so, in fact, you're the first one who's been invited since. And being the apothecary, I've been the only one allowed to leave the convent as well."

"It is a bit unusual for a convent to stop seeing anyone. Have you had the plague or something?" I asked, because although Monte Sacro was well-known to be a holy place, it was a wonderful breeding ground for diseases, too.

At this Sister Maria became a little uncomfortable. "No one really knows, although there are rumors," she said very quietly, as if the walls in the monastery had ears, as well as being damp.

"Ah, the joys of living in community, eh?" I chuckled. "Lay people seem to think we lose the ability to be human once we don the religious habit. Show me a religious house where they don't have rumors, or where they don't have discord, and especially where they are inoculated against doubt, and I'll show you a religious graveyard."

Sister Maria rocked with laughter, and said, "Oh, you're so right, Brother Julian. You are so right!"

"Let me know when Mother will allow a visit, and I will try not to embarrass you," I said, with genuine warmth for this special woman.

Whilst I waited to hear back from Sister Maria, I spent many a happy hour with my friend going over a project close to my heart, which was the preparation for the Christmas Mass. Although it was still several months away, if it were to be a truly joyous occasion, then the singing must be joyous, too. I love to sing from my heart, and I thank the good Lord that he has provided me with a sunny disposition. My friend and I went through all of the archives at Monte Sacro and discovered some hymns that hadn't been sung for quite some time, yet would resonate with joy when properly sung by a group of well-rehearsed monks.

The next morning, a message arrived from the convent inviting me to join them for their midday meal. As I walked into the little piazza and looked up at the imposing dome of the grand church that dominated it, I was happily humming some of the tunes we had rediscovered the day before. Just then a little voice caught my attention, saying "I've seen you wiv Dom, ain't I?" whilst giving the official greeting of such little ones, which was to wipe his face with the tattered sleeve of his jacket.

"You're a very observant young man," I said whilst reaching into my pocket for the crust of bread that I always carried to give to such as him.

He sized me up and down as he hastily ate the bread that I'd given him. "You looks an honest man," he said, then added "for a monk anyways"— a compliment I found difficult to decipher.

"It appears that you know who I am, young man," I replied looking around to check that no prying eyes were watching us. But the windows of the convent didn't face onto the square, as the building was hidden behind the massive edifice of the church itself. "Have you seen any unusual visitors come in or go out of the convent?" I asked.

"Depends by wot yer mean by 'unusual.' To such as us, they is all a bit unusual," he retorted with unexpected insight. "The fing is that this ain't the best place to look fer anyfing unusual anyway. If you ask me, if you want to shift summink wot you don't want uvvers to see, then yer'd use one of them tunnels wot runs out of there from the cellars underneaf." Giving me the ritual sniff of urchin intelligence, he continued. "But the good news is that there's more of us than there is of them," jerking his thumb in the direction of the convent, "and I reckon we's got all of them exits covered." His grubby face grinned.

"How would you know where those tunnels ended?" I asked with genuine amazement.

"Who do you fink cleans the chimlies around 'ere? And who 'elps the rat catcher collect the dead bodies what 'e's poisoned and which's fallen down in places where big people can't get inta?" he informed me. This information made me wince with humiliation at what our poor discarded infants can end up doing. "Grown-ups don't fink we see fings when we're doing them 'orrible jobs, but we do. And we tell our friends, too. All of us little 'uns know which 'ouses 'as tunnels wot goes back and forth from that convent. And guess what, bruvver? Every one of them 'ouses 'as a little servant girl or boy what tells us 'ho's a coming and 'ho's a goin' in and out of 'em. You just tell Pietro not ta worry, 'cos we won't let 'im down." At that point my conspiratorial friend ambled off across the square with his hands deep in his pockets, whistling loudly.

"That's a beautiful tune," I shouted after him. "Can you sing as well?" He just turned and smiled. "Mebbe I can, and mebbe I can't," was all he said. He was about to continue on his merry way when an idea entered my head. "Hang on a moment!" I shouted again and hurried across the piazza to him. I whispered the idea into his ear, and he listened with a serious face, across which slowly spread a broad grin. "Gotcha," he said, tapping the side of his nose. "Leave it with me," he finished, and ambled off around the corner whistling like a lark.

Knocking on the big door of the convent resulted in a spyhole cover being slid to one side, and a wimple-covered face appearing in the barred gap. "Brother Julian," I announced. "Reverend Mother is expecting me," I said, at which point the cover snapped shut, and I was left communing with an ancient wooden door for some minutes. Whilst I was humming the hymn, "Knock and it will be opened unto you," the ritual of entrance to the convent began with the drawing of several heavy metal bolts and the creaking of ancient hinges. I was surprised to be met by a young woman who blushed when she saw me.

"Welcome, Brother" she said, and indicated that I should enter. "We don't get the pleasure of many men here." Her eyes darted to my face with a nervous smile. "Mother said to take you straight into the refectory, as the meal is ready to be served." I followed my guide's rustling habit along dark, dank corridors half-lit by high, dirty windows. She turned frequently to look at me with that nervous half smile on her sweet young face.

"This must be a cold place in winter," I commented. She giggled, which confused me. "I mean that it must be a hard place to keep warm," I muttered.

Before she could answer, we arrived at the refectory. All the Sisters were lined up along a trestle table, with at least a dozen down each side and Mother sitting at the head of the table like a hawk hovering over her prey. She indicated a vacant place on her left side that had been reserved for me. I was relieved to see that on my left was Sister Maria, whose eyes were demurely cast down towards the table.

I went and stood at my place. Mother inclined her head towards me and peremptorily asked, "Would you be so kind as to sing grace for us, Brother?"

I closed my eyes and paused for a moment, thinking of what would seem most appropriate for such an occasion. The silence in the room was tangible. Then I smiled to myself as I remembered a wonderful thanksgiving psalm, and sang those sweet and wonderful words. It took only a minute or two, yet when I stopped, the silence was still as intense, yet it was a silence full of light and repose. I opened my eyes to find all the Sisters had turned towards me and every one was smiling.

"Sit." The word crashed through the moment, and the tense atmosphere again snapped shut around us. The food was simple. There was no talking, just the scraping of knives on pewter plates and the occasional scrape of a foot on the floor. Eyes secretly darted from place to place, but Sister Maria kept her eyes focused on the table all during the meal. Mother rang a light with her thick hand, and all the Sisters rose as one. "Would you like to visit the Chapel, Brother?" Mother asked, in her crisp, clipped voice.

"Thank you, Mother," I replied. "The food was delicious." This last comment was met with a slight raise of one of her eyebrows as she turned and left the room, with me following behind like a lost schoolboy. The transition from those dank grey corridors into the chapel could not have been more stark. Inside that holy place, it was all gilt and glister, stained-glass glories, and sensuously carved dark woods with the patina of the many souls who had passed over and beyond them.

"It's beautiful," I said with genuine admiration, "and I would think that the acoustics are wonderful too." I turned to Mother and said, "Do you mind . . . ?"

"Certainly," she said. And I hummed some arpeggios before launching into some of my favorite hymns.

"Perfect," I said, with a big smile on my face, which sadly was not reflected in her face.

"My office." I was beginning to think that she was afflicted with some sort of illness that only allowed her to say two or three words together. But she had already genuflected and was leaving the chapel. I followed obediently.

Mother's room reflected her personality to a tee: austere and cold with a pinched feeling about it. "I was honored to be asked to join you for a meal, Mother," I said, in my most genial of voices. "Do you often receive guests here?" I asked, veritably oozing with friendship and light.

"Our vocation is to serve our Master by doing what we can, Brother. But as a rule, we don't encourage people to join us as we have to be busy about our Father's work." She made the sign of the cross in an automated fashion.

I stared around the room. "This hasn't always been a religious house, has it?" I asked, gaining the courage that a full stomach often brings. "I'd heard it was once the home of a less-than-Christian banker who came to a bad end. And I hear tell that there are cellars underneath that are linked by dark passages to other houses where darker deeds were done in times past. Just imagine if those walls had mouths as well as ears." I paused for a quiet chuckle to myself before suggesting in a conspiratorial tone, "I bet they could tell some strange stories, eh, Mother?" A slight color came to her face, or perhaps it was the contrast with the whiteness that now edged her aquiline nose that made her face seem pinker. But she never faltered from looking at me straight in the eye.

"As a rule, Brother, we don't listen to gossip and fairy tales. We have better things to do with our time," she retorted.

"But we religious love our mysteries, don't we?" I pushed her, "And would you believe that just the other day a rumor reached our own humble house that strange things had been seen coming and going at this very convent in the middle of the night. Do you think it was ghosts or fairies or just local tittle-tattle?"

The slight color on her face disappeared as the pupils of her eyes darkened like an impending storm.

"Brother Julian," she said in a glacial voice, "it does you no credit to repeat such offensive gossip. You may close the door as you leave." The iciness in the room was nearly tangible.

"Thank you, Mother," I replied in the most polite manner I could summon up, then turned and left, trying to look as monkish as I could.

As I walked away from her room, I saw the welcome sight of Sister Maria in the corridor. One would almost suspect that she'd been loitering there, but the mere sight of her dissolved any arctic memories associated with her Superior.

"What a joyous sight to a lonely monk," I said, trying to bring some cheer into such a cold and isolating place. She turned and showed me her face, and her intelligent eyes seemed to reflect how I felt. And I must admit that it had a most strange effect on me.

"It's good to be able to thank you for coming, Brother Julian." Just hearing her say my name made me feel as if we'd been friends for a long, long time. "One more thing," she added, looking swiftly behind her at the door to Mother's office. "On occasion I'm called into the community to see a sick person." She paused before saying, "Perhaps we could meet. There's something I'd like to tell you about."

"I shall have to return to my chapter in Rome soon," I replied. "Now I'm feeling so much better—thanks to your expert ministrations, dear Sister—there is little reason for me to remain at Monte Sacro."

"Expect to see me or hear from me soon, then," she said. "If I can't leave, then I'll send a message to your house in Rome. Blessings and good-bye, dear friend." And she lowered her head and walked away from me down that dark, dank corridor.

I returned to the nearby monastery, where I stayed for two more days without hearing back from Sister Maria. Having run out of excuses to remain at Monte Sacro, I made the return journey to Rome on a bright, sunny day and determined to stop off at brother Gian's taverna for purely nutritional reasons. I paused along the way to buy some flowers from a beggar woman just outside the Porta di Roma. Bringing a small gift to my little niece was a long-standing tradition.

There were three or four customers enjoying the hospitality of the house: eating the food, drinking the excellent wine, and of course talking in loud voices with each other. Gian was very pleased to see me as he'd begun to get worried, not having heard from me for several days.

"You've grown thin," he said, staring at my ample girth, "what happened to you out at that swamp of Monte Sacro?"

"Oh, I got caught in the rain and then came down with a fever. But I was well attended to by a delightful Sister from that convent we have an interest in. Sister Maria's her name," and even as I said it, I felt a strange flush rise up in my cheeks. "Oh dear," I hurriedly added, "maybe it's still lingering with me." Gian gave me a knowing look, which I realized would be foolish to comment on. "But getting well gives one such a wonderful appetite," I said, to which Gian replied, "Well, some things never change, eh? I'm glad to hear you've recovered, and I'm even happier to see you in the flesh—even if there's not as much as there was last week!" And calling out to his wife in the kitchen, he said, "Julian's here and he's in need of a good feed. Bring some pasta and some wine to help give the man some strength back." Then he stuck his head into the store room and called for Dom to see if he could find Pietro. "Tell him that Julian's back," he said, and gave further instructions that we should all share our news before I returned to my duties at the Church.

Soon, the three of us were seated at a round table, enjoying the delicious food Gian's wife had prepared for us and sipping wine from his well-stocked cellar. Wiping the food from my face, I began to hum to myself again, and it came into my mind that I hadn't hummed like that since I'd left Rome. I was just starting to reflect on that when Pietro walked in, accompanied by a deeply grimed urchin with a very intelligent face.

"This is the Bishop," said Pietro. The young urchin wiped his nose on his sleeve before nodding at each of us and saying "Salve." He stared around the room for a moment, but it was the food that attracted his fullest attention. Gian, knowing how empty a young boy's stomach can be, went into the kitchen and returned with a mountain of pasta surmounted with steaming sauce. He placed it in front of the urchin.

"Thanks, Signore," were the last two words we heard for several minutes, whilst he proceeded to shovel the pasta from plate to palate.

"I met one of your friends up at Monte Sacro, didn't I?" I said.

The Bishop nodded, but continued eating.

"I hope the message I gave him had some effect."

Here the Bishop paused to smile, nodded once more, and again continued eating.

"I'm lost," said Dom, looking from one to the other. "What message? Where?"

"I'm sorry, Dom," I said, "Perhaps I'd better fill you in. My trip to Monte Sacro was to find out if our friends were still being held there. Obviously Reverend Mother wasn't going to invite me down to give them my blessing, so I thought I'd play the ferret instead."

"Now you've completely lost me," said a dejected Dom.

"Hunters send ferrets down holes to chase out rabbits. The Bishop's confrere told me that the cellars of the convent are connected to a veritable rabbit warren of tunnels that lead to surrounding houses. So I whispered to him what I intended to do, and he, knowing where those tunnels ended, was going to put his ragged band of guards on the alert to see if anything or anyone popped out on their end."

I then finished with a sweetly sung "I have led my people out of bondage," and emptied my glass of wine.

By now, the Bishop had finished his pasta and was wiping his plate with a large chunk of bread. The rest of us were bemused to see him glance longingly at the food scraps left on our own plates.

"Perhaps before your stomach busts, you'd better tell us what you were telling me on our way here," chuckled Pietro. Our hearts warmed at the sight of the satisfied smile on the young lad's face.

"Thanks, Signor Gian. Tell your donna that I've just eaten the best meal of my whole life. But if there happened to be a little dessert left over somewhere, I just might be able to squeeze in a taste," he said, with a sly wink at Dom.

"You'll go far," was all the Dom said. But he said it like a proud brother.

"Well, as I was saying afore I was interrupted by this tasty repast: Bruvver Julian 'ere is telling the truth when 'e said that my bruvvers was waitin' at all them 'ouses where them tunnels end, and lo and behold, yesterday evenin' just a'ter sunset, that old cart rumbled up to one of them 'ouses. Two fellas in big cloaks 'nd 'ats goes up to the front door, knocks on it, and after a while they disappears inside. About ten minutes later, one of 'em pops 'is 'ead out the door and 'as a quick look-see. "e's got some steel in 'is 'and is calling to 'is mate that s'all clear. Then the next bloke leads out two wimmin and three little 'uns all blindfolded and tied to one anuvver. The blokes bundles 'em on the cart and 'eads off out inter the countryside. Needless to say, there's a few little shadows following 'em. Any sign of that dessert, Gian, mi ol' friend?" He grinned.

The four of us were a little taken aback by the news, but it was Dom who first spoke up, "You said there were *two* women, Bishop?"

"Tha's right, Dom—two wimmin. But yer not gettin' any of me dessert for bein' so smart."

"And only three children?" added Pietro.

"Well, give the man a coconut! Wha's wrong wiv you all? You all sound like a bunch of parrits!" the Bishop said. "And Gian, ol' fella. Mi dessert?"

Still there was no movement amongst the four of us, and the young urchin threw up his arms in mock disgust before folding them across his chest. But like all good homes with a woman in residence, the needs of the child had been heard. Gian's wife appeared with a bowl of fruit topped with thick cream: "Just to fill those gaps . . . ," she said with a warm smile.

"Thanks, Signora," said the Bishop, focusing with renewed relish on the bowl before him.

"It doesn't make sense," said Pietro, "they must have been mistaken. The other woman must have been Marco, but then where was the other child?"

The same thoughts were buzzing around in my head, stubbornly refusing to settle into any sort of clear pattern or reason. There was something I was missing. I believed the Bishop, because he was a sharp-witted young lad and hadn't let us down in any way so far. So why *two* women, and why a missing man and child?

I was tapping out a tune on the tabletop when a terrible thought struck me like a physical blow. Gian noticed my sudden quietness and looked at me with concern. "Are you okay, Brother?" he asked.

"Just give me a moment, please," I answered, "but I think I have the answer to one of those mysteries— although I pray to the dear Lord that I'm completely wrong." And pausing to take a sip of wine and to offer up a few silent aspirations, I regathered my senses. "When I was up at Monte Sacro and came down with a fever, an apothecary was sent from the convent. Her name was Sister Maria and she was very kind to me." I paused for a moment, and my friends waited for me to continue. My heart seemed to race within my chest, and my head felt light. I struggled on. "I met her again up at the convent, and she said she had something to tell me and hoped to call on me before I left, but she didn't." By now my heart was threatening to burst from my chest and I was forced to pause once more. "I am beginning to think that someone overheard that conversation, and that she is the other woman who was bundled onto that cart." Gian came around the table and put his arm round me as I covered my face, and my shoulders shuddered with half-suppressed sobs. "She was such a very kind Sister. It would be cruel if anything happened to her just for wanting to talk to an old fool like me," I said, striving to regain my composure.

Pietro was turning his beads through his fingers all this time and trying to make sense of all that he heard. "It certainly would fit the facts," he conjectured, "but until we know where that cart was heading and who was in it, we're all still very much in the dark. Bishop, is there anyone still watching those houses up at Monte Sacro? Because if Marco and a child are still unaccounted for, then they'll have to come out sometime."

"Don't you worry about nuffing, Pietro. My people are on it, and my friends is sharp as tacks when it comes to watchin' you adults." The Bishop buried his head in the food once more.

"Don't make yourself sick by eating too much, Bishop," said a concerned Dom.

"A growin' lad needs his victuals, Dom. Look at youse. You must've packed it away when youse was a little 'un."

Dom smiled and ruffled the young ruffian's hair. "If I were a guessing sort," he said absently to the others present, "then I'd have to say that I think that it's Clare who's the missing child. It fits with her history. Remember how Rosso was told never to ask who her mother was? Well, perhaps her mother has found out who she is and has decided to take matters into her own hands."

"That's what I was beginning to think, too, Dom," said Pietro. "But what's happened to Marco, then?"

"All we can do is wait for the Bishop's friends to come back with their news," I said, having recovered my equilibrium. "And I must say all this adventure and emotion gives one a serious appetite, eh?"

"Are you 'aving a piece of me, Bruvver?" asked the Bishop with his streetwise smile.

"Certainly not. It goes against the ecclesiastical grain to do something like that! Now dear brother Gian, there wouldn't happen to be a little bit of that glorious pasta left in the kitchen, would there? I will have to go soon, and only the Lord knows when I'll get a morsel of food to eat again."

"I will go straight away and check for you, Brother. We can't have you fading away to nothing, can we?" As he turned, he gave those gathered a conspiratorial wink.

We stayed on for a short while before we departed and went our separate ways: me to the monastery, Pietro to his solitary room, and the Bishop to only he knew where. Within a very short time, I was back in the routine of the Church's life, with sung Matins and Vespers and Mass during the day. In addition to singing, I was in charge of the music collection, which was stored at Santa Maria Maggiore. The vast, illuminated books were kept in a special room in tall cupboards to accommodate their great size. Each sheet of music was a work of art, and I treasured the fact that I was the one who had the privilege of taking down those folios and being able to leaf through them. Each piece of paper told a story, as well as denoting the music inscribed upon it: music that reflected a glory beyond our limited use of words.

I immersed myself in my music and my prayers and remembered especially Marco and his family, and my new friend Sister Maria. I wondered what had become of them.

Laura's
STORY

SISTER MARIA CAME into our rooms in the basement of the convent, and the door was bolted behind her. Since we'd been brought here, we'd only seen her and another young Sister who had delivered our meals. They were obviously sworn to silence and the other one had dutifully obeyed her superior. But Maria was different. She'd seen us when we arrived and asked if we had been treated well and if we were in good health. She had kind eyes, and the children had taken to her immediately. But when she entered on this occasion, she was without her veil. Her close-cropped hair gave her the air of someone persecuted and alone.

"We didn't expect to see you, Sister," I said. "How long are they going to keep us here, and why are we here, anyway? We've done nothing wrong."

"I don't know," was all she said, as she slumped down into a chair and burst into tears. I looked across at Marco, who had the children behind him in the corner. Whenever we heard anyone outside our door, he immediately herded them to the corner so no harm could come to them unless the person got past him first. And it would take a mighty man to get between Marco and his children. But the sudden appearance of Maria, without her veil and seemingly locked up with us, too, only deepened the mystery.

I crossed the few paces that separated us and put my arms around her shoulders and let her sob her fears away. Soon she stilled and wiped her eyes. She sniffed and wiped her nose, and when all anguish had been wiped away, she looked straight at me and said, "I'm Connie Maria della Rovere, and up until a few moments ago, I was Sister Maria di Angelo, the apothecary at this convent. It appears that Mother Superior has decided that the company I keep is not conducive to remaining in a Holy Order, and so she has stripped me of my veil and sent me to join you as special guests of the convent down here in the basement." As she said these words, a whimsical smile began to appear on her lips.

Marco looked at me and shrugged. Since we'd been bundled out of the forge in the middle of the night and brought here, this was the longest conversation we'd had with anyone, and even though she had an innocent and true face, it crossed my mind that perhaps she'd been sent here to spy on us for whatever reason our captors had.

Maria reached out her hand and held mine as if she'd been reading my mind and said, "Perhaps if I tell you why I think I've been locked up with you, it might ease your mind. You know Brother Julian?" And at the mention of Pietro and Rosso's friend, we glanced at each other and relaxed a little. Marco came and stood near me, but still placed himself between the children and the door.

"We know Julian," interjected Marco. "What's your connection with him?" he asked with a slight edge remaining in his voice.

"How do I know him?" she said. "He has the voice of an angel and the gentle heart of a good and pure man. I met him the other day, and I think he knew you were here. He came to the convent to have lunch with us. He and I secretly planned to meet so that I could tell him about our 'visitors' in the cellars, but someone must have overheard me saying that I would contact him and obviously jumped to the correct conclusion. I think that's why they decided to lock me in here with you."

"Who are 'they'?" asked Marco, who had plainly decided that Maria was telling the truth.

"I'm not sure. Whoever they are, they must be very powerful, because not many people can upset Mother's equilibrium, and she's been shaken by this whole affair. Brother Julian really rattled her when he intimated that he knew you were down here," she replied. "But exactly who 'they' are is still a mystery to me. Tell me," she said, smiling kindly at the children who had begun to play a game in the corner, "who are you and why did they bring you here? Perhaps that might cast some light on this dark mystery."

I felt Marco's little finger entwine itself around mine and felt great comfort from the warmth of it. The air of tension and sadness in the room had gone, and now we felt strengthened by a new and blossoming friendship with a fellow traveler on an unknown path.

"We're just a normal little family who lives next to the piazza near Santa Maria Maggiore. Marco here is the blacksmith, and these are our children Sarah, Clare, Rizo, and Bini. We know Brother Julian through our friendship with Brother Rosso and Pietro, who often visit our house. A few nights back, we'd put the children to bed after a normal day's work. We'd gone to bed as usual when there came a banging at the door. Marco looked out of the window and saw two men below with a cart. They said Cardinal Borgia's coach had broken an axle and that it was needed for urgent business. Marco called down that surely it could wait until the morning, because even a Cardinal needs sleep. But they kept banging on the door, and so he went down. I turned over to return to sleep when there was another bang on the door, and then another. I went to the window, and the two men were still there with their cart, and Marco lay on the street at their feet. 'Your husband seems to have tripped and fallen, Signora, perhaps you should come down to help us with him.' I threw some clothes on and rushed down and knelt next to dear Marco." I paused in anger at the memory of it all, but Marco's hand gripped mine more tightly and whispered, "It's OK, just tell Maria the rest of it."

One of them grabbed me and said that if I wanted Marco to be unharmed, then I'd better bring the children down, too, because we were going on a journey. I was beside myself with fear. I suddenly thought that Marco might be dead already, but thank God he stirred. He's a tough man to kill. And even now, just thinking about it brings tears to my eyes.

I went upstairs and gathered some clothes. Then I woke my little sleepyheads up and told them we had a surprise for them: we were going on an exciting journey, and they should get ready as quickly as possible because it was going to be such fun. The girls were great, but the boys had to be pried from their bed and carried downstairs." Again I paused, but my anger was rising. "Those terrible men tied scarves around their mouths and then threw sacks over their heads. We were lashed together like cattle and pushed up onto the cart and lashed up tight under the canvas. We had no idea we were in a convent until your Sister appeared with food the following day." A slip of my hair caught in my lips, and I paused to remove it.

"Are you alright, Mamma?" asked Sarah from the rear of the room.

"Yes, darling," I replied, "Come here and meet Sister Maria. You, too, Clare, and that includes you, too, boys. The bare-headed nun held out her arms to embrace them all, and they happily fell into her arms.

It was as if they'd known Maria all their lives, and they proceeded to give her a hug and then a kiss on both cheeks.

"Thank you so much," said Maria. She turned to me and said, "You have beautiful children! Are the girls twins? They look the same age to me."

"Clare came to us a little while back. But she's one of the family now, and we all love her being a part of it." Marco had crept up behind them and had his arm around Clare's shoulder.

"She's a very special part of our family. Brother Rosso brought her to us when she was abandoned in the piazza. Her father's dead, and we think her mother is, too. But our family is very blessed to have her as a daughter and a sister."

Maria looked at them all with a gentle sadness in her eyes. "Thank you for having the faith to share that with me. I know I'm a stranger to you, and I am—or was—a Sister in the community where you've been imprisoned. And that's the terrible truth, because that's what really happened to you. You're prisoners here. I have no idea why, but someone wants you kept locked up, and they've locked me up, too, because they heard me talking with your friend, Brother Julian. So I'm afraid my good intentions have come to naught!"

"Don't worry, Sister," said Sarah with her serious voice. "Mamma and Papa will look after you, won't you, Papa?"

"Thank you, Sarah" replied the nun, with a warm smile playing at the corners of her lips. "I am sure that with the protection of your Papa and Mamma, everything will be fine. And don't forget dear Brother Julian. Now Mother suspects that he knows you are here, I'm sure all of this will be cleared up shortly, and you'll be back home before you know it."

We'd all begun to feel at ease with each other and soon the children were sitting on Maria's knee as if they'd known her all their short lives. Marco and I sat in a corner and enjoyed the scene.

"I don't know what's going on," said my loving husband. "If they were going to kill us, why haven't they done so already? And why these comfortable rooms? It's not as if we've been thrown into dungeons or anything, and even the food has been good enough to satisfy a very hungry blacksmith." He smiled at me with those gleaming brown eyes of his.

"We keep coming back to that little word 'why,'" I said. "You think it's something to do with Clare, don't you?" And he simply replied, "I do. Rosso told us all about Villeprieux, but he was always very close-mouthed when it came to talking about Clare's mamma. Do you think he was hiding something from us, too?"

"I'm not sure, but I think you're right. Whatever the reasons behind it all, we must protect the children and be strong for them," I said.

"Don't worry, Mamma," said Sarah from behind a chair. "We'll be fine." And both Marco and I burst out laughing.

We didn't laugh for long, though. There was a rattling at the door as it was unlocked, and in came Mother Superior, accompanied by four irreligious-looking men in long cloaks. "These men have come to take you to your next destination. I am sorry that we've had to keep you locked up like this, but it was for your own good," she said in her clipped, sharp voice. Maria stood tall and never flinched from looking at her. "But you have to make a decision." Marco and I instantly locked our fingers together and braced ourselves for some bad news. "You cannot travel together. We have to break you into two groups," she said, struggling to tell a lie, "as there isn't enough room in the carriage for all of you. So you and you will go in one carriage and the rest of you will travel separately."

The two she had picked out were myself and Clare. Marco stood forward immediately and said, "you will never separate my wife from her children unless you kill me first." The four men looked at each other and braced to advance on him. But Mother spat out an icy "No" and lifted her arm to stop them. "There will be no blood spilt in this house." In the tense seconds that followed, I exchanged a glance with Marco, and he indicated that he would go with Clare, and I would go with our children.

Mother seemed to have come to a conclusion. "So be it," she said to Marco, "you will go with Clare, and the rest will travel separately."

My family instinctively gathered in a tight huddle. I noticed Maria standing to one side, isolated and vulnerable. I waved her over into the welcoming embrace of our family. "It's going to be a bit strange," said my good man, "but we will make the most of it all as long as we keep true to each other. Be good for Mamma until Clare and I get back to you, and remember me in your prayers every night."

"Daddy," said Rizo, "are these men 'bad men'?" We all turned and looked at them. As we did so, one blushed uncomfortably, and the others stared at Mother and tried to avoid our gaze.

"I think they're just doing their jobs, Rizo," Marco said. "And sometimes following orders can be a very hard thing to do, eh? Like washing your hands before meals." And his powerful arms drew us together as we smiled at what he'd said.

"I'm sorry," said Mother Superior, "but you must come now." Marco held me tight, and in that moment, I tried to imprint in my memory the feeling of every part of his body, the warmth of his breath against my cheek, and the scent of his hard body, all familiar from every day of my married life.

Then Clare came to me and held me close. "It's alright, Mamma, I'll take care of him for you. We'll be fine." My throat tightened, but I was determined not to cry in front of them. The children hugged their Papa and smothered Clare with kisses. Sarah whispered final instructions into Clare's ear. And then they were gone.

Two of the men led them away, with Marco carrying Clare in his arms. My last memory of that moment is the touch of Marco's little finger as it gently entwined itself with mine.

Maria came and stood next to me with the other three children close in front of us. One of the remaining men indicated with his head that we should leave, whilst the other went on in front. As we passed Mother Superior, Maria paused and said quietly to her, "I forgive you, Ann" and moved on without waiting for a reply. It was probably the first time in many years that the poor, frozen soul had been called by her real name, and I prayed that her heart would be softened by the memory of it.

"Did you see the size of that man's dagger?" said Bini to Rizo in a very loud stage whisper. And the guard of whom he spoke couldn't suppress a smile as he marched on in front of us.

We were led down long, dark passages with other black-mouthed openings telling of other passages going in other directions. The man in front held a burning torch above his head. The torch spattered dark spots of tar on the dark and dank walls. We finally came to an open doorway with dancing light beyond it from other torches. We went up the narrow stone stairs on the other side and came into what looked to be a scullery. The recesses of the room glinted with pans whilst the lingering smell of the previous evening's cooking haunted the space like a friendly ghost.

The door to that room was unlocked by an unseen hand, and we went out and down along a garden path with the night stars remote and pure in the heavens above. A dark carriage loomed out of the darkness, and we were bustled inside and the door secured. There was a sudden lurch, and we moved off. I had my arm around Sarah and Bini, whilst Maria hugged Rizo close on her lap.

"Do you think we'll see any robbers, Mamma?" asked Rizo from the safety of Maria's arms with barely suppressed excitement. It was difficult to be cross with him, so I quietly answered "I doubt it, Rizo. Not when we've got you and Bini to protect us."

It was a long night, and we dozed between jolts. Although the city is quiet at night, the noises of the countryside are quite different, and we soon realized we'd left the city behind. Dawn found us many leagues distant from the city and heading north toward Florence. We stopped shortly after dawn at a small village to break our fast and were let out of the carriage. Our guards were surprisingly courteous and made sure the innkeeper provided us with all the food we desired. From that point on in our journey, we were allowed to have the carriage windows open so that we could enjoy the sights of the countryside as it slowly marched past us.

"Where do you think they're taking us?" asked Maria.

"I've no idea," I honestly replied. But inside all I could think about was where they had taken Marco and Clare and what might be happening to them.

"Don't worry about Papa," said Sarah in her prim-and-proper fashion. "He's a blacksmith, and there is no one stronger than him in the world. And I told Clare to never leave his side, otherwise he might get very upset."

"I think you're probably right," was all I could find to say, between my desire to laugh and my inclination to weep. We continued to rock our way north, skirting the large towns and stopping where we could to change horses and attend to our essential needs.

"Why Clare?" Maria asked out of the blue during one of those long periods of time when the mind becomes numb with the monotony of what it is seeing. It seemed unfair not to tell her, and to tell you the truth, I was happy to share my thoughts with someone else. So I recounted the story of how Clare arrived at our home after Rosso had found her abused and abandoned in the piazza. Of how it had taken some time before she'd come to accept Marco, and then hearing of the terrible things that had been done to her when she'd lived with foster parents. Of the mysterious reason Rosso went to Paris, and why he had taken Clare with him in search of her French father. And how it turned out Villeprieux, a friend of his during the time he wandered the highways after running away from home, was her real father. But of her mother nothing was known, and Rosso never talked of the mother at all.

All these things I shared with Maria, and we both moved to the conclusion that perhaps it was the link with Clare's unknown mother, long undisturbed until Rosso appeared in Paris, that had stirred up this current turmoil. "But why separate us? Why not keep us all together where they can keep an eye on us all? It doesn't make sense," I said.

"I may have lived in a convent for some years, but I come from a minor noble family, too. And believe me, there is a great deal of intrigue with those powerful ducal families. I wouldn't be surprised if we haven't become some pawn in a bigger plan," said Maria, then she suddenly laughed. "But those ducal families have nothing on the intrigues that go on inside some of our Holy Church institutions! Look at me! Sister Maria one day, Concietta da Montefeltro the next."

"I thought your name was Maria," I said, somewhat astounded at this news.

"Maria was the name I was given when I entered. My real name is Concietta Maria da Montefeltro. Maria is my confirmation name. But when I was little, everyone called me Connie. In fact I'd be really pleased if you'd call me that, because it's the name my Mamma used when I was young."

"Did you hear that, boys?" I said gaining the attention of my two young bandits who were shooting imaginary arrows at brigands on the trail. "Maria's real name is Connie."

"OK, Mamma. OK, Connie" was all we managed to get out of them as they continued to slaughter the enemy in a new shower of arrows from their imaginary bows.

From the direction we were headed, I thought perhaps we were going to Perugia, but the carriage detoured around it and then continued in an easterly direction.

"Do you think they're taking us to Ancona?" I asked Connie with fear in my voice. Ancona was a port from which ships traveled to the Orient, and people were traded like cattle. Connie held my hand and tried to reassure me that all would be well, and why didn't we ask our guards as they seemed like reasonable people.

As the days had drawn on, our guards had relaxed more and more and had even begun to indulge the boys with games of bows and arrows during breaks—and often falling dramatically into the dust clutching an imagined lethal shaft in their chests. After waiting in a deathlike pose that would entice Rizo and Bini towards them to see if they were really dead, they'd leap up and chase the boys around the carriage with much screaming and laughter. The guards' names were Antonius and Nicola. They were simple young men just doing what they had been told, even though guarding women and children was not why they had joined up as soldiers. They were sons of small farmers from Marche, and the land their fathers worked was too small for all of their sons to make a living off of, so the two had been sent off to become soldiers. It was the first time that I had heard the name Cesare Borgia mentioned, and it troubled me a lot. But Nicola and Antonius spoke of him with great admiration. They spoke of his daring feats as commander of the French forces that had won so many battles around Italy. They spoke of his courage and his deep loyalty to his father Pope Alexander. And they spoke of their confusion as Cesare had seemed to change after the defeat of the Sforza family in Milan. But that was a world away from where they were now, halfway to their homeland of Marche and the real hope of seeing their dear parents, brothers, sisters, and all the little children that had no doubt appeared whilst they'd been away.

"It looks like we're going to Marche, then," said Connie to Nicola.

"I'm sorry, Connie, but I can't tell you that," he said with a smile, "but I'd be lying to a nun if I were to tell you we weren't," and gave her a wink that made her blush.

"They should never let young soldiers near women," she said, straightening her habit and unconsciously brushing her cropped hair into place.

"They're harmless," I told her. "Mind you, there are many that aren't. But I think we'll be safe in their charge. It's what happens after we get to where we're going that worries me." I automatically looked around to check that my little brood was in sight.

"There must be a reason why someone like Cesare Borgia would take a harmless little family and an ex-nun hostage and move them away from Rome to Marche," said Connie. "But I'm blessed if I know the reason why."

"I think the most important thing is to say as little as we can and to accept whatever it is that comes our way," I said, and then called the children to me. "Sarah, Bini, Rizo: listen to me for a moment. I know we're having fun with Antonius and Nicola, but when we get to where we are going, it may be that there are other people who might not be quite as nice." And holding them close, I continued, "Some of them might even be cruel to us, and others might try to be our friends just to get information out of us."

"What's information?" asked little Bini.

"It means they might want you to tell tales about Papa or Clare," I answered, and before he could air the thoughts that were forming in his mind, I added, "but we must always be loyal to them and if anyone asks you anything about them, just tell them to talk to Mamma."

"Does that include me, too?" asked a somewhat crestfallen Sarah.

"I'm afraid it goes doubly so for you, young lady," I said. "It will become immediately apparent to them that you are a very knowledgeable member of our family, and they will almost certainly try to weasel information out of you if they can. All I'm saying is think before you speak and, if in doubt, then ask them to talk to me." With that little sermon finished, I gave them all a big hug and sent them off to play whilst the two men changed horses for the final leg to Marche.

"Laura," said Connie to me quietly. "I need to tell you something about myself." She'd said it in such a confessional sort of way that she immediately had my attention.

"Go on," I replied, reaching for her hand.

"You know that I told you that my name wasn't Maria, but Connie Maria della Rovere?"

"Yes," I answered with quiet interest.

"Well, it would probably be wise not to tell anyone else about that. You see, Cesare Borgia drove my uncle, the Duke Guidobaldo da Montefeltro out of Urbino and, how shall I put it, they don't exactly see eye to eye. And if Cesare knew that the Duke's niece was riding into his town unannounced, well, he might not be quite as kind to us as we hope." With that, she gave me a wry smile.

For some reason, I laughed softly. "It's at times like this that I thank God I married a simple blacksmith." And Connie smiled back happily at my understanding of it all. "I don't think the children will have noticed you telling me your full name so there's no need to trouble them with that. But what will you do now? Be a nun or be a lady?" Connie looked out the window of the moving carriage, but I don't think she saw anything that passed in front of her eyes.

"You know what Laura? I think perhaps that's the wrong question to ask." And giving me a wide smile, she said, "You'd be very surprised to find out how many of my Sisters at the convent didn't act like ladies most of the time. I think," she continued in a measured tone, "that perhaps I will live the life of a nun within the world and not locked behind cloistered walls. I know some orders already do that, but in my heart I need greater freedom than most religious orders allow me to have."

"Go on," I said, intrigued at her line of reasoning.

"I really feel very deeply in my heart that I do have a calling to follow our Lord, and that makes me very happy, and I could easily continue to stay as a nun. But when I met Julian—and he's such a beautiful man with such an incredible gift—something inside of me changed a little. Please don't misunderstand me," she added, her face coloring a little, "there could never be anything like THAT between Julian and me. But I saw in him something that we share, and that's having a gift that we really want to share with others for their benefit and not for our own. His great gift is music, my lesser gift is to bring healing and caring to those who suffer. And although the habit affords me certain respect, it also cuts me off from many of those who need me most."

I looked at this shorn, exiled nun in the remnants of her habit and felt humbled by what she had shared with me. Surely this was a gift of love just dressed in another form of clothing. Marco and I shared a love that had filled our life to overflowing with joy and had blessed us with our beautiful children. But how many more people would Julian and Connie touch with their unique and generous gifts.

"You are a very special lady, and I am honored to call you friend, Connie. Allow me to be your companion where I can and to help you in whatever way you would like me to." Then we embraced and smiled at one another.

"There's a huge castle over there, Mamma" said Bini, with eyes the size of saucers, "an' there's soldiers with huge spears riding on great huge enormous horses, too."

"That's Urbino." said Connie. "That's where my family came from. They're not there now as Cesare has chased them into exile, but there are probably still people there who might recognize me and that could prove difficult for all of us."

"When were you last here?" I asked her.

"I was sent to the convent when I was 10," she answered.

"Well," I smiled back at her "I think that this shorn-headed, intelligent, confident lady looks dramatically different from a shy 10-year-old. And I doubt that Cesare will have let any of your family's servants stay on, from fear one of them might poison him." Connie relaxed a little at that thought.

"Perhaps," she said after a pause. "Let's just pray that you're right, Laura."

"But before we get there, we need to get you out of your habit and into the spare dress I brought with me. We can rip your old clothes into rags and drop them out the window as we go along."

"We can use them, Mamma," shouted Rizo. "We can make capes and masks for when we get there just to show them that we're soldiers, too."

"For a boy," said Sarah, "that's an amazingly intelligent idea. Come on," she said, "I'll show you how to do it properly."

When our carriage stopped outside the palazzo at Urbino, three ladies of varying heights stepped out, followed by two small, stern, bodyguards dressed in black capes and black masks, which made even the craggiest of attending guards smile with amusement.

We were led up the steps of the palazzo and taken to a suite of rooms towards the back of the building. They were light and airy and had a good view of the surrounding countryside, but the sound of the lock being turned from the outside reminded us that we were prisoners and not long-looked-for guests. The children had the greatest of fun exploring the apartment for hidden panels and concealed trapdoors, and all three squealed with delight whilst jumping on the large double bed they'd decided would be theirs to share at night.

Connie and I also made a round of the rooms and to our delight found that there were spare clothes already to be found in a large chest in the second bedroom. A knock came at the door, and the lock was undone.

"Enter," I called out as the children gathered around us. A swarthy man of short stature who sported a very serious expression came in and bowed slightly to us.

"I hope you find your accommodation to your satisfaction, ladies," he said. "I see you've found the change of clothes in the trunk," he added, glancing toward the open chest and the scattering of clothes around it. "Although we had been told to expect only one lady in the party."

"Signore, none of us expected to be here," I interceded, "and we would sincerely appreciate an explanation as to why we were kidnapped from our home, held hostage in that convent in Rome, and now dispatched to distant Urbino, cruelly separated from my husband and other daughter. Sister Maria here appears to have been caught up in this terrifying ordeal simply because she tried to get news of us to our friends, and for her pains has been thrown out of her community and into our nightmare." All this was said with rising indignation that seemed to have little effect on our jailer's icy exterior.

"Be patient, Signora," he replied in a condescending voice, "but thank you for explaining the presence of Sister Maria, who seems to be a member of a most liberated community, judging by the style of her dress." A slight smile flickered around the edge of his pencil-thin lips.

"If it comes to making remarks on how people dress, Signore, I would appreciate it if you would remove your muddied boots from the clean coverings on our floor." And we both stood there, staring hard at each other.

"My apologies, Signora," he said after a moment of silence, "it is good that you respect the splendor of your surroundings. I will tell the Duke of your sensitivity to your accommodation." And leaning his back against the wall, he bent down, pulled off his boots, and handed them out of the door, adding "Clean them!" to some hidden servant who was waiting on him outside.

"Now, down to business," he said, coming fully into the apartment and standing by the desk that faced the window. "You have full use of these rooms whilst you are guests here, and at certain times of day, you will be allowed free use of the gardens outside. Should you wish to go into the town, arrangements can be made to escort you. You may wish for your children to continue their education, and if that is so, then we do have the services of a tutor who can help them with their studies. Are there any questions?"

"Where is my husband?" I asked as politely as my emotions would allow.

"I am afraid I am not in a position to tell you that, Signora. But once my lord the duke has arrived, then I am sure he will inform you of the answer," he said, with all the emotion of a bored clerk performing a perfunctory role.

"Children," he said, "do you have any questions?" Although it did not show to the man, my mother's eye could see the great effort it took Bini not to utter one single word as the three of them stood there in polite, yet steely, silence. "Humph," he said, "I see. But when you are ready to talk, please just knock on the door and ask your retainer to call Consigliere Farinosi." And bowing once more, he left the room. And of course the lock turned once more to seal us in.

"What's a tutor?" Rizo burst out.

"And what's edu–whatsis?" asked Bini.

I looked at Connie and our faces mirrored each other's smiles, releasing the tensions of the previous few minutes. "It's a bit like making bows and arrows and using them to catch animals. But instead of making them out of wood, you make them out of ideas and use them to capture knowledge," I replied, with a certain smugness at the image created in my mind. The boys just looked at me with blank expressions.

"It means using that," said Sarah, giving then a pat on the head, "instead of that." And she tickled them under their arms, which led to a furious chase around the rooms accompanied by a great deal of screaming and laughter.

There was really very little we could do. Escape wasn't an option, and we had no means of contacting anyone to help us. Our only choice was to make the most of what we had and wait for an opportunity to make a plan.

That evening we asked for food and were brought a very presentable feast which we ate with relish, leaving nothing on our plates. When the servant came to clear away the platters, she let a little smile show on her face as if pleased that the food had been fully appreciated.

"Do say 'Thank you' to whoever prepared such a wonderful feast," said Sarah in her most polite voice, and for once, both boys joined in with a very loud "Thank you." It doesn't take much to make a Mamma proud.

"I'll be sure to pass your thanks onto Cook," said the servant over her shoulder.

We settled down for the evening, but as we were all very tired from the journey, we said our prayers early and went to bed with the setting sun. If Marco and Clare could have heard the prayers sent up to our Heavenly Father by his littlest children, their hearts would have been strengthened by the love that went up with those innocent requests.

The next morning I asked the guard to call for Consigliere Farinosi.

"Buon giorno, Signora," he said. "How may I be of service to you today?"

"Thank you for coming so soon, Consigliore. I am sure you have plenty of things to do for your master. We would like to take you up on your offer of a tutor for the children, and perhaps later this morning, we might visit your gardens, too?

"I will see to the tutor this very morning, and as for enjoying our modest garden, I will arrange for the gardener to attend to your wishes, too. Is there anything else that you need for your comfort?" He spoke all this in a much softer manner than he had used when we had arrived, and although I felt I could never fully trust him, I thought him to have an honest heart—albeit a heart under the control of a scheming duke.

"No," I answered with respect, "I think that should be all, thank you." And bowing once more, he left.

"Did you notice he'd cleaned his boots?" said Connie with a grin. "I don't think he's used to dealing with women."

"Mamma?" Bini interrupted.

"Yes, Bini?"

"What's a tutor?"

The tutor turned out to be an old man, clean shaven, with a long shock of white hair and bushy white eyebrows that had a mind of their own—much like their owner. He entered after a soft tap on the door, which Sarah opened.

"You must be Sarah," he said, with a polite and gentle incline of his head. "If I'm any judge of character, then I may not have much to teach such a bright young lady."

"Thank you, kind sir," replied my eldest, with a modest nod of her own head in return.

"Ladies," he said, turning to Connie and me and adopting a more formal bow, "allow me to introduce myself. I am Jacobi—often referred to as the Jew, and sometimes politely so."

I heard Connie's quiet gasp, and I saw Jacobi's quick clear eyes dart in her direction. There was no change in his attitude, but I saw in his eyes a fleeting look of surprise. "I am Laura, and this is Connie. I believe that your star pupils are the ones making that racket in the other room," I said, to gain his attention.

"It always helps to have a lively body and a lively mind if one wants to live a full life, my lady," he added, looking directly at me. "I have been blessed to have many such students over the years," he added, and even though he was looking at me, I knew the words were directed at Connie. He continued, "If my hearing is correct, my new pupils are hunting down bandits, and with a modicum of success, judging by the noise they are making. Believe me, Madam, in these times they will find plenty of bandits to chase in any Italian court." His smile spoke volumes, but he went silent.

I went to the door of the boys' room and ushered them into Jacobi's presence. They stood on either side of me as I introduced them to him. "Fine young lads and fertile ground, no doubt," he said, coming forward to greet them. "I am pleased to meet you, Bini and Rizo. No doubt we will learn a great deal from each other." He stood with a hand resting on each of their shoulders and speaking directly to me said, "We all learn in different ways and at different speeds. It will take me a few days to find out where their strengths and their needs lie. If the weather is clement, then you will find us in my school of life out there in the gardens. Then once we understand each other, I will start the journey of their enlightenment. Do feel free to join us at any time. After all, you are their first and best teacher." After bowing his head to me, he turned to Connie. and said, "Signorina." He held her proffered fingertips whilst looking closely at her face.

"Signore." Connie acknowledged him with a slight inclination of her head.

The boys glanced back over their shoulders as Jacobi led them out the door. Bini put his fingers to his lips and made a theatrical "Shh" sound. Even from the side, I could see a smile alter the old man's expression. As the door clicked shut, Connie whispered, "He knows me. He was my tutor when I was only very little, but he had a falling out with my uncle, and I thought him banished from the land."

"Will he keep quiet?" I asked her.

"I'm not sure," Connie replied with a furrowed brow. "Uncle treated him very harshly, but Jacobi was always very kind and patient with me. I don't think he'd done anything wrong, it's just that the Jews always seem to get squeezed when a war is bubbling somewhere. But he seems to be back in favor now, and he'll be an excellent teacher for the boys, too."

"What's it like being back here after all these years?" I asked Connie. We were sitting on the edge of the bed, looking out over the magnificent gardens below.

"It's funny," she began. "Everything seems so much smaller, and yet after convent life some things seem so much bigger, too. I always thought the garden went on forever, but when you see it from up here, it's not that big, really."

"Believe me," I interrupted, "it's a lot larger than the average garden you'll find behind a smithy's forge." Connie's face reflected my grin as she continued with her story.

"When my uncle was in charge here, I was pretty well left to roam the place as much as I liked. Being at the end of the family line and being a girl meant that not much was expected of me. That's why I so enjoyed my times with Jacobi. He taught me so much about the herbs and medicinal plants that were grown in the palace physic garden that it was only natural that I thought of becoming an apothecary. But most of the people who work in the palace are quite secretive. They have to be, really. If you say something that might be held against you later, then you'd be thrown out or even worse . . ." Connie looked sad as if remembering something that she'd rather not remember. "Powerful people can do some cruel things when forced into a corner."

"Do you think that's what happened to Jacobi, then"? I asked. Connie smiled.

"One thing you could always be certain of was an honest response from him on any subject. And, of course, he made many enemies. I suppose it was only a matter of time before one of them found an excuse to take revenge on him for telling the truth."

"Come on," I said. "Let's go outside and see what those boys are up to. And I wonder where Sarah has gone?"

In the days that followed, the palace seemed to absorb us into its daily routine. The weather remained sunny and warm, so much of our time was spent in the gardens. Sarah appointed herself as Jacobi's permanent assistant and followed him everywhere. "She is a very bright young lady, Laura," he told me one day. "In another world she would make a wonderful consigliere."

"Thank you, Signor Jacobi. She is a wonderful daughter, too, although I fancy she will make a great teacher as well, having practiced so much on her two younger brothers."

"You may well be right there, Laura," he said, with a dutiful inclination of his head.

Although our time in the palace was comfortable, Connie and I never lost sight of the fact that we were incarcerated there against our will, and we still had no idea of where Marco or Clare were. Then things began to change rapidly.

A messenger arrived early one morning, and all of a sudden, the palace was in an uproar.

"What's happening?" I asked the young man stationed outside our door.

"Pope's dead," he said, biting deeply into a crisp apple.

"The Holy Father?" I replied incredulously.

"The very same," he replied between crisp crunches of his fruit. "No doubt there'll be plenty of others lining up to take over. Always is, eh? They say 'is son is none too well, either," he finished, as he bit off another piece of apple.

I closed the door and went to tell Connie.

"The pope is dead, and Don Cesare is sick," I told her. Connie instinctively crossed herself and said a silent prayer.

"That'll set the cat amongst the pigeons," she said. "I wonder what Papa will do now?"

She didn't have to wait for long. The next morning an envoy arrived at the palazzo from Guidobaldo da Montefeltro, the exiled Duke of Urbino and Connie's uncle. Her uncle was coming back to reclaim his lands. Shortly after we heard this news, there was a light tapping at the door, which Sarah opened.

Her eyes lit up in delight and she said, "Come in, Signore," then over her shoulder to me shouted, "It's Signor Jacobi, Mamma," and ushered her wise mentor into our apartment.

"Good morning, Signore," I began.

"Good for some, but not for others, I suspect, Signora," he interrupted me. "I fear that I must leave in haste. No doubt you've heard the news about Signorina Connie's uncle returning to Urbino?"

"So you knew about Connie all the time," I said with feigned surprise.

"But certainly, Signora. A teacher never forgets one of his star pupils." Turning to place a hand on Sarah's shoulder, he added, "Your daughter reminds me so much of her." Jacobi looked very happy as he said those words, but his face soon clouded. "But I fear the Duke may not be happy to see me here, and I think it prudent to leave as soon as is convenient. Which will be this afternoon," he added as an afterthought.

"But where will you go?" I asked.

Connie entered the room then, asking "What's happening"? I explained all that had happened in the last few hours, and she sat down to consider what might be the best plan for us. Jacobi coughed.

"With your leave ladies, but I must be gone. Adieu."

"You can't just let him leave, Mamma," said Sarah with pleading eyes. "Where will he go?"

"Get me some paper," ordered Connie, and I did as she asked. She quickly scribbled a note and handed it to Jacobi. "You're to go to Rome, Signore," she ordered. "Give this to Brother Julian at Santa Maria Maggiore. Once he has read the contents, he will advise you what to do next. You will be safe with Julian." Pausing, she added with a slight color to her cheek, "He's a good man."

"Thank you, Signorina Connie." He reached out to hold her hand and quietly said, "I have always trusted you." He then turned and left.

"Where are those boys?" I asked Sarah. "Go and find them and tell them to come here at once." Sarah recognized the tone in my voice and immediately did as

I wished without comment. Turning to Connie, I said, "What do you think we should do now?"

"Pack," was all she had time to say before the thunderous sound of a hundred horses reached our ears from outside the wall of the palazzo. She looked at me with a wan smile as she went to the door and said, "I think I'd better go downstairs and meet Uncle, don't you?"

When the children returned, they were already aware of the arrival of the real Duke of Urbino. "You should have seen all the horses and soldiers, Mamma," said Bini, with his eyes as wide as saucers. "And they had HUGE spears, too," added Rizo, stretching his short arms as high above his head as he could.

"What's happening, Mamma?" said Sarah in her sensible voice. "And where has Connie gone?"

I explained everything to the children as best I could, and then fussed over them as they gathered their things together. The boys were delighted to put their black capes on, although even in the short time we'd been at the palazzo, they both appeared to have grown. "Look at you, Bini," I said. "Your Papa is going to be amazed at how big you've grown. You'll soon be able to help him out in the forge."

A troubled look clouded the young man's face "But what if I want to be a noble knight or an artist?" he said, "I'm not sure that I want to be a smith anymore." I crouched down next to him and looked him in the eyes.

"Every job needs men with good hearts, Bini," I said. "Whether he's a man who leads, a man who follows, or a man who shoes horses, we need those men to be good men. That's all your Papa wants for you, too. As long as you have a faithful heart, then we'll do whatever we can to support you in whatever trade you choose. But believe me, you will never meet the man who is the equal of your father, even if you were to walk to the other side of the world," Bini looked at me, and then my little son, my beautiful little boy, threw his arms around my neck and burst into tears.

"I miss Papa," he sobbed into my neck. "I miss him so much."

The sound of men walking down our corridor increased and then stopped outside of our door. It opened, and a tall man walked in. He was followed by two guards whose large frames almost obscured the small figure of Connie, who brought up the rear. I dropped a knee in front of him, and Sarah immediately copied my action. The boys just closed in tight against me.

"Signora Laura?" asked the Duke of Urbino.

"Yes, my Lord," I replied "and these are my children: Sarah, Bini and Rizo."

"Fine-looking children, eh," he said, taking the chin of each one in his hand in turn and studying it closely. "Father's a blacksmith, I hear?'

"Yes, my Lord. I believe he and my other daughter are being held hostage elsewhere."

"Hmm, yes. That's what my niece here has been telling me. Well, you're not of much use to me. Connie," he called over his shoulder. "What do you want me to do with these people?" Connie came forward and stood next to us.

"There is much work to be done in the city, my Lord Uncle, for the sick and the suffering, and I offer my humble services to you to help alleviate their distress. But before I do that, I ask that you permit me to accompany this badly misused family back to Rome to be united with the rest of their family. It may be that I can persuade Marco, Laura's husband, to return with me to Urbino, as there is much he could do to help restore the city after the recent troubled times."

"Always wanting to make the world a better place, Connie. If only there were more soft-hearted, good people like you about, instead of the hard-headed, selfish idiots I have to deal with most of the time. Be off with you, but please don't take my best horses. They're pretty tired after the gallop they've just had." Taking his niece in his arms, he said, "You always were my favorite," and he kissed her tenderly on her forehead.

"One more thing," Connie said, as her Uncle's eyes rolled up towards heaven.

"With a woman there's always one more thing. Go on. What is it?"

"Money?" she said.

"Give her what she needs and no more," the Duke said. Spinning around to leave, he added, "and don't

loiter in Rome for too long, or I'll miss you too much."
Then he was gone.

Connie went to the door and called after him "Thank you, Uncle. I love you, too." His fading voice replied, "Come back soon."

Marco's
STORY

SMITHING IS A patient business. When I was a young lad, I suppose that I was like most young men and very impatient with the world. But working with iron changed all that. I remember the first time I tried to make a horse-shoe with my Papa. I put the iron in the fire, pulled it out far too soon, and banged on that iron until my arms ached. All the time my Papa watched and never said one word. When my arm was so fatigued I could hardly raise the hammer, he quietly took it from me and put it on the edge of the forge. He took the bellows and blew air into the coals until they were a gleaming red. Then he took my piece of iron and put it in the hottest spot and sat down in the sunshine.

"All it needs is a little patience," he said and put his head against the sun-warmed wall and whistled softly to himself.

He knew his iron. He knew what patience was. And he knew how and when to use his strength. When he was ready, he plucked the glowing iron from the fire and placed it on the anvil.

"You try now, son," he said, and stood back to watch.

Even though my hand was still red and stinging from my feeble earlier attempts, this time when the hammer hit, the softened metal sang and obeyed my commands. It was a lesson that I've never forgotten.

Most men can become very strong, but not many men know how to effectively use that power. And very few powerful men know the meaning of patience, which is why they never achieve great power.

But as wonderful a teacher as my dear Papa was, it was my Laura who revealed the gift of love in me, and that is what really changed my life. The day she walked into my life and said not one word to me, my heart heard the story told since ancient times of love and beauty, of giving and cherishing, of gentleness and of commitment. She changed my world by completing it, so that when those men arrived in the dead of night and banged on the door, threatening our lives, my physical power was of no avail, but I knew our powerful love would endure all that came our way.

This was the thought in my mind when the convent guards slammed and sealed the door on the carriage that was to take Clare and me away. My arm may have been her shelter, but it was Laura's love that cemented our true strength.

"Where are they taking us?" Clare asked.

"Nowhere that we can't cope with," I replied, as peacefully as I could. "We just need to be patient until things become clearer. If they'd meant to harm us, I think they'd have done it already, so there's more to all of this than meets the eye. We won't know until we get to our destination, so why don't we just try and get some rest, eh?" And I closed my eyes and tried to remember the feeling in my little finger when Laura had last held it with hers.

The dark gloom inside the carriage cleared as our eyes became accustomed to it. Next to the driver's seat was a lamp that sent shards of light through the cracks around the door. We saw Mother Superior standing on the steps of the house, her face a soft yellow glow in the lantern light, and to me, there was a look of suffering etched into it. Then there was a slight lick of a whip, a whisper to 'Move on,' and we started to go. Mother Superior's image remained frozen in my mind as she disappeared from view.

We tried to make ourselves as comfortable as we could, and Clare nestled close into me in the cold of the night. Two blankets had been left for our use. I used one as a pillow and the other to cover us both so that we were cozy and warm.

"Have you ever been on a long coach trip?" Clare asked, obviously having no intention of going to sleep just yet.

"I went to Anzio once to do a job, which was quite far enough for me. Sarah had just been born and I really shouldn't have left her and Laura behind. But a job was a job in those days, and I couldn't afford to turn it down," I answered. "It's a beautiful spot, Anzio," I continued. Then added cheekily, "Do you think if we ask the driver, he'll take us there instead?" And Clare chuckled conspiratorially from out of her safe cocoon.

"Rosso and I went on a long carriage drive to Paris with Villeprieux when he was very sick," she said. Clare had never once mentioned to Laura and me that Jacques Villeprieux was her real father. As if reading my thoughts, she said, "I only knew him for such a short time, and I don't think he ever knew that he was my papa, which is very sad for him, don't you think?"

"He knew," I replied quietly. "Rosso told me that at the very end when he was with your papa, Rosso told him that you were his daughter, and that it made your papa very happy. Rosso said that your papa went to his Maker with that beautiful thought in his mind and great peace in his heart."

"Goodnight, Papa," said Clare. "I think I'll go to sleep now." And with those words she nestled deeper into my chest and fell fast asleep.

I thought back to those heart-wrenching times after Clare first arrived when she cringed at the sight of me. She now knew who her real father was, and yet she had chosen me as her Papa; I was humbled by her unconditional love.

Whilst Clare slept softly on my chest, I wondered how my beautiful Laura was doing. I felt some relief that Sister Maria was with her to help with the children. I knew Laura would cope with whatever came her way, and that no person or thing would daunt her. But the deep, dark doubt that someone would harm her or the children did not fully submit to my will until I hammered it shut behind an iron door in my mind.

I awoke to a sheet of white light flooding into the dark carriage.

"Alright," a voice said, "you can get out and stretch your legs. Time to change horses and get some food." And outstretched arms reached up to help Clare as I handed her down.

"Where are we?" she said, rubbing the sleep from her eyes.

"Not allowed to say," the guard said. "But if you go into that taverna, you'll find refreshments fit for a real Signora," he said in a civil manner.

I climbed down after Clare and eased my cramped limbs as I looked around at where we had stopped. We were on the edge of a small hillside village where life had carried on despite popes, emperors, and Caesars leading their armies up and down this track for millennia. I'd guessed that we were taking a northerly route and said to the other guard, "I haven't been to Perugia before. What's it like?" He was about to answer me when his friend shouted, "Remember what I told you about talking to our guests?" And he put his finger to his lips to demand silence.

I followed Clare into the taverna and sat down at the table, which certainly had a welcoming spread on its solid wooden surface. The owner of the taverna was trying to shut the door to the kitchen, from which sounds of slaughter were coming. "Chickens," he succinctly said. "One of them didn't want to die without a struggle" and gave me a whimsical smile.

"I know how he feels," I replied, and we both smiled in a friendly manner. "What's wrong with the door? Bad lock or bad hinge?" I asked.

"Both," he said. "I've been meaning to get it fixed for months, but with one thing and another . . ." He came over to us with some fresh baked bread, some fruit, and some wine.

"Mind if I take a look at it?" I said. "I know a bit about those sorts of things."

"Well, if you don't mind, my friend, it would be a great mercy to me and a great relief to my wife. She hates for the smell of cooking to linger here in the dining room and spoil our guests' appetites. But eat your fill first, and then have a look after that." So Clare and I broke our fast, and whilst she was finishing her meal, I checked the lock and the hinge. They had simple problems which I was able to help him with, and fixing them allowed me to see who was on the other side of the door.

The kitchen was a hive of activity with the tavern keeper's wife busily preparing the food for the day. She was short, square, and stocky, as are many good ladies in this country of ours. And like all good Italian women, she loved to talk. "Nice to meet at least one handy man in this house," she said, as she bustled around the kitchen. "Aldo said he'd fix that door last year," and she nodded toward the public area where Aldo was within hearing distance, and then threw her hands in the air in mock despair! "It's not often we get such fine visitors as you so early in the day," she went on, "you must have left in the dead of night from Rome." She gave me a knowing glance whilst she pummeled some pasta dough. "Your messenger came through yesterday morning on his way to Perugia and said to expect you. Are you her bodyguard?" she asked, with a quizzical eyebrow raised high.

"Less chat in the kitchen, my love. The gentleman don't need to have his meal spoilt by your tittle-tattle. He's kindly offered to fix our latch, so let him be in peace." She rolled her eyes heavenward at this statement and stuck out her tongue in his direction.

"I'd better finish doing what I'm doing and then get back to my little girl," I said. It was a simple thing to fix the lock and make it move freely on its hinges. Then I thanked the Signora for her kindness and her wonderful food and left.

"I hope those townsfolk in Perugia can produce as good a meal as you've eaten this morning. But knowing them, I doubt they will," she shouted after me. Our first guard shook his head in disbelief, whilst the other sported a satisfied grin.

The smile was swiftly removed from his face, however, as a sudden swirl of wind whipped the canvas at the back of the carriage, the leather fastener coming loose and striking the man across his cheek with a stinging 'thwack.' At this, his companion shrugged smugly and said, "Make sure you fasten it properly this time," and went to climb up front and take the reins.

"That hurt," his friend said, with real upset in his voice. He rubbed the red weal now rapidly appearing on his cheek.

"Here, let me help you," I suggested.

"Thanks, friend," he replied, and we went to secure the rear cover in the now-still air.

"Well, what have we here?" he said, forgetting for an instant the discomfort of his face. We both looked into the luggage area to see a dust-covered, half-starved little urchin who was fast asleep. "Well, I'll be . . . ," and his astonishment was interrupted by his leader, who shouted from his elevated position, "What's going on back there?"

"It's just a little kid stowed away in the luggage area," I shouted back to him. "He only comes up to your knees, so I don't think he'll cause you any troubles." At this moment, the little boy—for so he was—woke up, and the whites of his eyes were heightened by the grime on his face and the black rings encircling those sunken features.

"Who are you, and where am I?" he asked in fright, whilst receding into a corner like a cornered little beast.

"It's OK, my little stowaway," I tried to reassure him, "I'm Marco." The guard with me chimed in cheerily, "And I'm Antonio, but everyone calls me Toni."

"And I'm Clare," said a head that had popped up between the two of us.

"And if you don't clear of out of there before I've got my belt off," shouted the angry leader, "then I'll give you a thrashing that you won't forget for a long, long time."

I turned and stood in front of that ignorant fool and quietly suggested to him that such an action was not going to happen unless he wished to move me out of the way first. "You see," I said calmly, looking at his stubbly face, "You've taken my wife from me, and you've taken my precious children away from me, and now you threaten this small boy with violence. I'm normally a very peaceful man, but I, too, have my limits. If you lay one finger on that boy, I promise you that I will break every finger on both your hands so that whenever you try to do up your belt in the future, you will remember what a stupid fool you really are." And I just looked into those eyes of his and saw the little bully behind them.

He hesitated for a few moments before saying, "If he's not out of there in five minutes, he stays till we get to where we're going, and then see what happens to him." And pretending to give a fierce snarl, turned on his heel and went back to the reins.

Toni reached in and lifted him out, "What's your name, little friend?" he asked, as if they'd just met in the piazza.

"Coppino," said the little lad, in a dry, husky voice.

"Let's take him into the taverna," I suggested. "I'm sure the Signora will be kind to him if we ask her nicely." And so with Toni in front and Clare and I following, we went back inside and called for Signora.

"Mamma mia," she said, when she saw the little mite in such an exhausted condition. "Bring him into the kitchen where it's warmer, and we can get some food and drink into him." We followed her, and Toni set his light load down on a bench, saying "You be good now, and do as this kind lady tells you." And leaning down, he whispered into the boy's ear, "If you're still here when I come back down this way, I'll give you a lift back to Rome if you like." He gave Coppino a conspiratorial wink to seal the deal. Then looking around with some embarrassment, he added, "I've got lots of little brothers and sisters at home, and the kid reminds me of one of them. Still,

I'd best get back to the coach before Himself goes completely berserk." And with that he left.

Immediately Coppino said, "Marco. You know Pietro?" Hearing that dear man's name came as a complete surprise, and yet reminded me of a world that I'd only left a few days ago, but which now seemed like a lifetime away.

"Did you say Pietro? Of course I know him, but how do you know him?" I asked, in complete confusion.

"Tush tush," Signora butted in, "he can answer questions once he's got some nourishment into him," and the look she gave me reminded me why men think they run the world, but really it's the women that run our lives!

"I'll help him," said Clare, and the two children retreated to a corner near the fire. Signora bustled around preparing some food and drink for Coppino, and I stood guard by the door to intercept any disturbance.

Just as the boy was eating his food, there was shouting from outside the taverna. "If you don't come out here now, then we'll come in with swords drawn and that means someone is bound to get hurt, if you get my drift." It was the voice of our guard, who had rediscovered his power and sounded like he really meant to use it.

"Well, go on then," said Signora, "I don't want my home smashed up by those two ignorant brutes. I'll look after this little lad as if he were my own bambino." And ruffling Coppino's unruly hair—much to his great annoyance—she shooed Clare and me out of the kitchen.

"It's alright, Papa, Coppino and I had a good talk whilst he was eating. I'll tell you all the news when we're in the coach."

Toni shrugged his shoulders as we exited the building, but his superior was still sulking after I had forced him to back down. He harried the two of us as we climbed into the coach and made a big fuss about making sure the doors were securely locked.

The carriage danced forward with a loud crack of the guard's whip and we continued our journey to Perugia. "I think we're going to Ferrara," said Clare.

"Ferrara?" I replied, "Why would we be going to Ferrara?" There was a delicious look of intrigue in Clare's eyes that made me smile and say "OK, I promise not to say anything until you've finished."

"Well," she began, with breathless anticipation.

"Unless, that is," I interjected with impish humor, "I have a question to ask."

"Papa, will you please let me speak?" she said. Then adjusting her dress, she sat in the corner so that she could talk directly to me, and I must admit to feeling like a little boy being given a lesson. But in my heart I was very proud of her confidence.

"Coppino's friend, he's called the Bishop by the way, but he's much younger than I am," she added with a certain superior look in her eye. "Well, he's a friend of Pietro's, and he's the one who's been helping Pietro find out what happened to us. They've also been talking to Brother

Julian and the Dom, and they've been frantically searching all over Rome for us. Luckily the Bishop was near our
house when they kidnapped us, and it was Coppino and
his sister Lola who were sleeping in a doorway nearby,
and who the Bishop woke up and got to follow the cart
to the convent. Then Brother Julian went up there on
some sort of pretense and got into the convent and met
with that frosty Reverend Mother." At which point Clare
paused to a give a fair imitation of Mother giving one of
her haughty, frosty looks. "This must have put the fear of
God into her. And I think it was then that she suspected
that Sister Maria was part of the plot against her and that's
why the Sister was bundled in with us. But the really in-
teresting news is that the guards who first captured us
are in the service of Cesare Borgia." At that, she folded
her arms across her chest in triumph and sat staring at
me with a look that said 'You do understand the impli-
cations of that statement, don't you?'

I am a blacksmith and the music of hammer on metal
is a steady, slow beat, but it gets results with persistence
and accuracy. Perhaps that's why a woman's mind is a
bit of a mystery to me—apart from my beloved Laura
that is. She knows my pace, and it seems to suit us. But
she sees and understands things that are a riddle to a
simple mind like mine. She calls it female intuition, and
even just saying it, I can see her face and the small smile
creeping around her lips as she says it. "Where have they
taken her?" I said to myself, staring at my impotent, cal-

lused hands. But I must have said it aloud because Clare continued with her conclusions from her conversation with Coppino.

"Remember when Rosso and I went to Paris looking for news of my parents?" she said in her lively, bright manner.

"Of course I do. And do you remember the look on my face when you came home again?" At that, she threw her arms around my neck and said from the comfort of my coat collar, "Of course I do, Papa. Of course I do."

"Well, dear, Rosso was so kind to me, and he tried to protect me from all sorts of things, but as Mother Superior in the convent in Milan said, 'Men aren't very good at hiding the truth from us women.' So of course I found out that Villeprieux was my other Papa, but he abandoned me and never even bothered to find out where I was. Not like you, Papa—he was nothing like you." And again she nestled into me and the power of love that had grown between her and the rest of the family breathed a freshness into that darkened, bouncing coach. "Did I tell you that I met his uncle, too, my great-uncle?" I nodded. I knew the whole story and it was safely stored in my heart. "I know he told Rosso that he must never ask after my mother because that would put us all in danger. But when he talked with me, he told me that he'd known my Mamma when she was the same age as me, and that he could see which side of the family I took after. He also said that she was a good woman who was in a very difficult position, and that she had been sorely used by her father and her brother. But perhaps one day things might improve, and then—and only then—she might send for me."

By this time Clare was sitting on the seat next to me, holding both my hands and staring earnestly into my eyes. "If I'm right, Papa, then we're going to Mamma's house, and her brother is holding Laura, Sarah, the boys, and Sister Maria at his castello in the Marche."

I stared into those perfect, innocent, yet intelligent eyes and let the clang-clang-clang of my slow wits reach the only possible conclusion. "So that means the Holy Father is your Nonno. Now I understand why Cardinal Villeprieux said it would be very dangerous to know that."

In the silence of our minds, ideas flashed in and out of our consciousness, whilst outside the sound of the metal-rimmed wheels striking flint from the road seemed an eternity away.

Ever since we had been taken hostage—for there was no doubt in my mind that was what we were, hostages—I had thought of escape. It would have been so simple to overpower those two guards and disappear into the countryside. But then what would become of Laura and the children? And now that I knew they were in the hands of Cesare Borgia, a man with a cruel reputation, the dangers we faced seemed small compared to what might happen should Clare and I escape. Our only hope lay in the fact that Clare's Mama, Lucrezia Borgia, appeared to have sent for her. The pope's daughter was often talked about in the marketplace and not all of it was to her advantage. But some said that with this last marriage and her removal from Rome, that she had become a model duchessa in Ferrara--and if she had any of the traits of her daughter, then perhaps there was hope for us all.

The journey continued for several days as we headed north and then east across the hills to Ferrara. Toni was a simple man who lived in fear of his fellow guard, but I could see that he was trying to be kind to us, and so we returned the compliment. When his companion jeered at his slowness of wit, we made sure to always thank him for his small kindnesses, even though they sometimes led to a cuff around his ears.

We were approaching a large city and had stopped at the top of a hill. Clare asked Toni if this was where we were going to. "No, little lady, but we're not far away now. That's Bologna. We'll stop there tonight and get to where we're going tomorrow."

"Stop your jabbering and tighten those girths, you lazy good-for-nothing," his companion shouted, flicking his whip at him. The tip of the whip was a bit too close for poor Toni, and a deep red slash opened up on his face. I stepped down from the carriage and went to the lad's aid. "Get back inside," roared the wild man from his high perch, "or I'll give you a whipping you'll never forget."

I may look slow. I may move slowly, and I may even think slowly, but when a man's daily job is dealing with scorching heat, sharp flakes of fiery metal, and the sudden jerk of a terrified beast as it's being shod, then he knows when to move quickly and has very fast reflexes indeed.

So I stayed firmly in place with my hand on Toni's shoulder and dared his companion to strike me. He raised his long leather whip, gleaming and shredded with overuse on innocent flesh, and watched it arc with geometric beauty toward me. I smiled, remembering the times we lads had played games in the stables where we'd learned our craft and had often played "will or the whip" with each other.

At the last moment, I shifted my weight and grabbed that vicious leather weapon and pulled hard. The guard, who was totally unprepared for such a movement, suddenly found himself in midair and heading back to earth with nothing to hold onto. Winded from the fall, he lay gasping for air whilst I cared for Toni's wound. By the time the guard found his feet again, I was back inside the coach with my arm around Clare. We were looking out the window, which I had decided we should have open to celebrate the final installment of our journey.

"Thanks, Master," said Toni, as he walked past the window. "I don't think the boss'll try that again, do you?" Toni winked and winced at the same time.

The Castello Estense loomed out of the grey curtain of mist that covered the plains surrounding Ferrara. Like a giant out of some fairy tale, it towered over us in the dripping silence. As we passed through the gates and into the town, familiar sounds met our ears: the sounds of carts moving over cobbled stones and shouts from vendors at the stalls in the small piazzas along our route. Then I heard a sound that caused me to put my head out of the window and look about for its source.

"Civilization at last," I said triumphantly to Clare. "There's a smithy back there," I explained, with a happy feeling in my heart. She looked at me for a second and smiled back at me. The town was alive with workers, and new buildings seemed to be going up everywhere. The Cathedral Church of Santa Maria soared into the misty heavens, whilst its great doors suggested a dark, mysterious cavern inside. We were driven straight to the Castello Estense with all its imposing fortifications. "A great deal of iron work has gone into that building," I said over my shoulder to Clare, whose chin was now resting on my shoulder as she, too, peered out of the window with increasing delight.

"I wonder where they'll take us, Papa? I hope it's not some dreadful dungeon." And although she only said it in mirth, my heart froze a little. But we needn't have worried. We stopped at a side door hidden halfway down one side of the Castello and climbed down from the carriage. A servant ushered us respectfully in through the door, up some stairs, and along a long, wide corridor festooned with paintings that were alive with color and form. Finally our escort stopped before an ornate door. It was opened for us, and we entered into a very comfortable apartment.

"Someone will be here to see you soon," said our minder. The door closed, but there was no sound of a lock turning. Being inquisitive, I tried the handle, and the door opened smoothly.

"May I be of service?" said our escort, who was now ensconced next to the door.

"No, it's OK. I was just checking." I smilingly retreated and closed the door again.

Meanwhile Clare had begun a tour of inspection. She had found a bedroom with a very large bed and was now bouncing on it.

"Look at me, Papa. Have you ever seen such a huge bed in your whole life? And the sheets are made of silk— and have you seen the gilt around all the mirrors?"

"It certainly is nothing like home," I replied "but for all its glitz, it's still our prison, and we shouldn't forget that."

"I know, Papa, and I haven't forgotten Mama or Clare- -but just imagine what Rizo and Bini would do in a place like this." Her eyes fairly sparkled with mischief!

"Let's have a good look around and see what we can find. You start in here, and I'll check out the other rooms," I said conspiratorially. And we parted on our separate voyages of discovery.

It didn't take me long to tire of all the glitz and excess in that pampered apartment. Mirrors, silks, even what I think was ivory abounded—but nothing of real use, to my eyes anyway.

A knock on the door disturbed us.

"Come in," I called out, and a young lady entered. She bent her knee slightly and murmured quietly, "Beg pardon, Signor but La Duchessa asks that you follow me, please." Clare took my hand before the maid turned and led us out the door. We followed her through the passage and up a staircase that was more accustomed to the steps of servants than of lordly people. At the top, she paused by a low door, produced a heavy iron key, and opened the lock. The open door revealed the rouge reverse of a heavy curtain, which she pulled to one side.

"Come in and wait here," she said in that soft voice of hers, then disappeared through the far door of this comfortable antechamber.

"Do you think we'll see my other Mamma?" whispered Clare.

"I don't know," I honestly replied, looking down into her brightly animated eyes, "I only wish Laura was here to shine a light on all of this mystery."

"I must apologize for all the mystery. But I'm glad to see that you've arrived safe and sound." The words were spoken by the lady who had silently appeared through the far door. At the sight of her, my thoughts froze.

She wasn't the most beautiful woman I have ever seen: my Laura is that woman. But this woman was still very beautiful, and her soft oval eyes barely concealed a raw animal power hidden deep inside her. She induced great wonder in the observer, and yet the faintest hint of fear as well. Such a mixture can be very intoxicating for any man!

Lucrezia D'Este, for that was the name she gave to us, held me in thrall and for a moment, I felt my whole body shiver. But then she released me from her silent hold and turned to look at Clare.

"What do they call you, child?" she asked gently.

"'Clare,' Signora," she replied, whilst curtseying politely and reaching up to hold my hand.

"And this is your Papa?" she said, with the faintest of pauses before the word 'Papa.'

"Yes, Signora."

"Do you know who I am?" continued the Duchessa.

"No, Signora," said Clare, whose hand was becoming increasingly moist in mine.

"We will get to know each other well soon," she said, coming forward to take Clare's other hand, "but first I must have a word with your Papa." And with a slight movement of her head, she indicated to me the door she had entered through. "Just wait here a minute, my dear, I won't keep your Papa very long." Looking at me with her grey, flirtatious eyes, she added, "Lead on, Signore."

The apartment on the other side of that little door was sumptuous. So many things in that room dazzled my eyes, leaving me bereft of any comprehension of what I was looking at.

"It's very pretty, isn't it?" the lady said, as she came and stood close beside me. For my part, all I was conscious of was the rustle of her silk dress, which reminded me of the soft swirl of leaves in springtime. I was also aware of the musky, feminine scent that came from her body, now almost pressing against mine. She came and stood right in front of me, gazing at me with those misty, beautiful grey eyes of hers, and said, "Do you find me attractive, Signore?" As she said this, she reached out and lightly touched my cheek. Every muscle in my body responded to the lightness of her touch. She must have read the re-action in my face because she moved closer, until I could feel her breasts touch my chest. I found myself intoxi-cated at the intimacy of her body as she slowly reached her hand behind my neck and slowly arched her head up towards me.

Her little finger dug into my flesh as she pulled my head towards her own, and it was that touch that brought me back to reality and saved me from a treacherous and foolish fantasy.

The last time I had felt the touch of a little finger against my flesh had been when Laura and I were parted from one another.

The lady immediately sensed the change in me and paused. "What is it? Are you afraid of being seduced by me, Signore?" Her grey eyes still smoldered.

"Yes and no, Milady," I smiled back at her. "I am honored by your attentions. Forgive my impertinence, but I am just a humble blacksmith with a wife and four children whom I love and care for. I am sure that there are many men who are far more worthy of your attentions than I." And lifting my arms up to release her grip from my neck, gently let them down until we were just two humans holding hands and facing each other, as normal people so often do.

As I looked at her face with clearer eyes, I now saw faint lines, and once again her look changed ever so slightly to reveal a glimpse of what might even have been fear. But it disappeared in a flash, and now she looked at me questioningly. "Your wife is a very lucky woman, Signor Blacksmith. Very few men would refuse the attentions of Lucrezia D'Este if they knew what was good for them." But there was no malice in her voice, which surprised me. "So Signor Blacksmith, tell me, what name do they call you when you are a blacksmith and not the almost-lover of Lucrezia D'Este?" By now, her eyes were giddy with fun as she turned her back and retired to a seat in the mullioned window.

"Come," she airily ordered. "Come and sit by me. We have some things to discuss, and we mustn't keep the girl waiting too long because these children have suspicious minds. I know, because I am a parent, too." And she tapped me on the thigh in such a playful manner that I was forced to smile.

I looked at this enigmatic lady for a brief moment to consider whether I should trust her, and felt that she was worthy of my trust: "My name is Marco, and my wife is Laura, and we have been blessed with three wonderful children. And of course you would know that Clare has been brought up as our daughter ever since she was found abandoned in the local piazza."

"Ah yes," she said quietly, "Brother Rosso. Tell me, what has happened to Brother Rosso? He seems to have disappeared from the face of the earth."

"You are well informed, Milady," I replied with quiet surprise.

"When you have lived the sort of life that I have, then all information is precious: but it's a weapon that can cut both ways. Be warned, Marco—if I know about Rosso, then others will surely know, too." Her hands were now formally clasped together in her lap, and she looked down at them before going on: "And no doubt on your journey here you've given thought as to why I—shall I say—summoned you?"

"I'm just a simple blacksmith whose duty it is to love and protect my family, and I will do everything and anything to make sure they all stay safe. Understanding the mind of a lady whom I've not previously met is a gift I have yet to master." I said these words quietly and firmly and without rancor.

"Wisely said, Marco," she replied. By now we were feeling our way towards each other in hoped-for friendship, and neither power nor passion would help us.

"You are a good man, and Laura is very blessed to have you for her husband. But for me, this is my fourth marriage and still I have yet to find the type of love you share. There was a man once, a long time ago . . . ," and silence filled the room. She shook her head as if emptying out some cluttered memories and said, "We will talk more later, but for now I want the two of you to feel very welcome here. My lord the duke is away at the moment, but no doubt he will already know of your presence and will want to meet you when he returns. Alphonso is, how shall I say, a little formidable when first meeting him, but if he likes you, then you will have no better protector in the whole of Italy. In the meantime, make yourself as comfortable as you wish, and perhaps you and Clare will join me this evening for a meal."

"We will be honored, Milady. But there is one question that I must ask before I leave: where is the rest of my family?"

"They are safe for the present," she replied with well-chosen words. "Apparently my brother Cesare decided that he needed what he calls 'insurance' against any unforeseen alliances that could affect his . . . er, inheritance." She looked at me as she said that, and I recognized the look of a kindred soul who was trapped by circumstances. Her expression changed again, and she said, dare I say with great honesty, "perhaps in a different time in a different age, it would have been good to know Marco, the blacksmith. Before he was married, of course," she added, and that impish twinkle returned to those beguiling grey eyes.

"Perhaps it would, Milady," I replied, "perhaps it would." And I kissed the tips of her proffered fingers as she held the door open with her other hand for me to rejoin Clare.

The sound of the door being locked behind me was the signal for Clare to unleash a torrent of questions.

"Whoa, my precious one. One at a time, and anyway, you'll be able to ask as many questions as you like this evening because we're going to dine with the lady of the house." Clare's eyes opened wide, and her excitement was tangible. She let out a small whoop and clapped her hands as she spun around. Then she hurled herself upon me saying, "Oh Papa, you are the best and bravest of all papas in the whole world. How lucky we are."

"Come on," I said, taking her by the hand and leading her back towards our apartment, "we have the rest of the day to explore. But remember Clare, this is a gilded prison, and Laura and the family are locked in another such as this, but a long, long way away. We may appear to be free to come and go as we wish, but we will be watched, and things could change in an instant."

"But what's she like, and what did the lady say about me?" she asked, with all the enthusiasm of youth.

"I can honestly say that I've never met a woman like her before in my life. In fact it was like meeting several different, intriguing women all wrapped into one in the space of a few minutes. I think it'll take me some time to work out which one she really is. But leaving all that aside, I think she's a good-hearted woman who wants to do best by those she loves." I stopped halfway along the corridor leading to our apartment and said to Clare, "I think she really wants to know who you are. And once she's found that out, she's going to love you just as much as Laura and I do."

"Thank you, Papa. You're the best Papa in the whole world!" And we hugged each other close.

For a man who's always eaten with his family around our own kitchen table, I'd expected that eating with the duchessa would be a grand affair with servants, pages, and general hangers-on. We'd tidied ourselves up as well as we could for the duchessa, and I'd helped Clare brush her hair, having watched Laura do it several times in the past.

When Clare placed a fine silk ribbon in her hair, I thought she looked like a princess and proudly told her so.

"For a blacksmith, Papa, you brush my hair beautifully," she said, with a lovely smile. "And you are definitely the most handsome blacksmith I know, too." Then taking my hand, she and I followed the servant girl to our repast.

The room where we ate was small and intimate and was in the same wing as the rooms where we'd met the duchessa earlier. She hadn't arrived as yet, and so we were left waiting by the open window, which let in fresh eddies of air from a gently darkening evening sky. Birds sang and swooped around the turrets as they searched for their muddied nest tucked high amongst the ramparts.

"It looks so beautiful from up here, doesn't it," I said to Clare, without daring to take my eyes off the beautiful vista.

"The voice of a poet, and the hands of an ironworker. What an enigma you are, Master Blacksmith. Or may I call you Marco now?" The duchessa had silently appeared in the room and been observing the scene before her. From the serene smile on her face, it appeared that she liked what she'd seen.

"Marco it is, Duchessa," I replied, moving to bow in obeisance.

"Please no, Marco. There's no need to be formal when we're alone, please just call me Lucrezia." And turning to Clare, she reached out both hands and said, "Welcome Clare. You cannot believe how long I have waited for this moment. Come, sit at table with me and we can eat and talk at the same time. There is so much I want to hear about you, and perhaps you might have a few questions for me, too." And that impish twinkle reappeared in her eyes.

"Marco, you sit on my right, and Clare, sit here next to me on my left."

And with that we sat down like a little family at a normal mealtime—except that this table was covered in an embroidered cloth of rare fineness, the plates were of silver, and the glassware the best that Murano could produce! Lucrezia was dazzling in a shimmering dark silk dress that reflected some of the grey from her eyes.

It was a high-necked dress, and her jewelry was remarkable for its absence. Her long golden hair was tied back almost severely behind her head, but her face radiated happiness and hope.

"Firstly, my little Clare, I have to ask your Papa for his forgiveness for the trials I put him through earlier." Clare looked at me questioningly as my face reddened to match the sinking sun in the velvet blue sky. "But don't worry, your Papa is a rare man and worthy of the name 'Papa,'" and she unconsciously reached out and gently placed her hand on mine for a fleeting second.

"And you, Duchessa, are a formidable woman and worthy of every man's respect," I said.

"A good answer, Marco. But please call me Lucrezia. I think we have entered a place where friendship lives and the rules of trust and honesty order the language we use." A servant appeared with simple food of cheese, olives, tomatoes, fresh bread, and oil. "I have good spring water if you like, or would you prefer wine? I'm told that it's very good," she said to us both.

"Water will suffice for us both, thank you," I replied. When the servant had left us alone, Lucrezia asked whether I would say the blessing over the food.

"Mamma usually says it at home," said Clare, "because Papa says the same prayer every time," and she gave me a knowing wink across the table. We all laughed at that, and Lucrezia suggested that perhaps Clare might like to say the blessing instead.

"Father," she began, "thank you for this food that you have provided for us to share and eat. Thank you for Papa and Mamma and all the family. Please keep them safe wherever they are, and do tell the boys to behave. Thank you for" and here she paused, opened one eye and said to Lucrezia, "What shall I call you?"

In that pause, a thousand things would have flown through Lucrezia's mind, but she replied with tranquility, "Perhaps you should call me your godmother."

And closing her eyes once again, Clare finished her prayer whilst the two adults looked on with humbled hearts.

Food was passed from one to the other, and the conversation that started with fits and starts slowly gained a life of its own. Soon there were tears, laughter, and moments of dense silence where only friends can pause in peace.

Our evening of happy sharing was shattered by loud noises outside of the door, which was flung open to reveal a travel-worn man whose dark hair, eyebrows, and beard had been grimed grey by the dust of the road.

"So here you are, my doting Duchessa," he roared across the small room. "Plotting something nice for your husband's return, eh?" Lucrezia never batted an eyelash at this unexpected onslaught.

"You're home early, my Lord. We weren't expecting you until tomorrow. Would you like a drink of wine to clear your throat? All that dust makes it sound so very grumpy."

"Of course I'm grumpy," he replied with vigor as he reached out for the proffered silver cup. "It's your bloody brother again. Up to his old tricks and trying to wriggle out of the snake pit he's created for himself. And who the hell is this?" he said, draining the cup to the very dregs in one swift swallow.

"This is Clare," she said quietly, trying to calm her very agitated spouse. "She's my goddaughter, and she's here for a visit with her father Marco." At the mention of my name, I stood up and bowed my head toward the Duke.

"Never seen him before in my life, and what with your bloody brother . . ."

"Please, my Lord," Lucrezia begged him, "Please. Not in front of the child."

"I'll say whatever I want, wherever I want, in MY bloody palace," he roared back at her. "And seeing as your bloody brother has stirred up such a shitstorm, it seems strange to me that these so-called visitors arrive at such an unusual time." He eyed me with such a villainous look that I averted my gaze. "Look at him," he roared again. "Bloody shifty eyes, too. Take him down to visit my brothers," he said, with a leering look that didn't speak much of brotherly love.

Lucrezia stood up straight away, her chair making a discordant scratch on the wooden floor. "He's my guest, my Lord," she said, with regal power ringing in her voice.

"I know, my dear," her slightly subdued spouse responded. "Once I am certain of his story, then I will welcome him as a . . . ," and here he paused before adding with a smile "as with your goddaughter. In the meantime, he can spend time with the rest of the family, eh?" And clicking his fingers for the guard, he said, "Take him away."

I was escorted from the room, leaving the duchessa white with rage, whilst her husband flopped down into a chair and called for another carafe of wine.

I was marched along corridors and down narrow stairs, and as we descended further, windows disappeared, and a cloying dampness began to seep into the air we breathed.

"The Duke's brothers don't appear to have a room with a view," I remarked to the guards who frog-marched me forward. But my wit was met with silence.

We finally arrived at a small room with a flickering oil lamp that cast a sulfurous light. There was straw on the floor, and in the middle stood a low oak table blackened from years of abuse. Behind it sat a squat man with pale skin and close-set eyes. His oily black hair was held in place by an even oilier black bandanna, yet there was a familiarity in his expression that tugged at my mind.

He merely grunted once his eyes had flicked over me and indicated to the guards that they should follow him. He opened a low, dismal door behind him and lifted the torch from its rusting iron ring. The torch spattered flaming fuel around him, which he ignored. Stopping outside a heavy wooden door studded with great iron nails, he reached for the keys hung from his thick leather belt. He squinted in the light to check he had the correct one, before yelling through the door, "Stand away." He then proceeded to unlock the rusted ironwork that sealed this living tomb. Hinges squealed at the insult of being awakened from their long slumber and reluctantly let the heavy door swing open. An awful smell assaulted my senses, and I was roughly shoved through the opening into this claustrophobic hell.

Strangely enough, my eyes accustomed quickly to the gloom of the cell. I looked up to see a high, narrow opening in the massive walls, with an iron grill that bled a thin moonlit sky into the dismal dungeon.

"Welcome to our hell, stranger," said a mocking voice out of the darkness. "Did my beloved brother send you here to keep us company or to further your education?" And he laughed an icy laugh, which sent a colder shiver through me than the one produced by the air in that awful place.

As my vision pierced the gloom of the recess where he sat, I saw him raise his fists and shake the shackles that secured him. "Pretty, aren't they?" And his thin, manic laugh echoed off the stone walls once more. "My regal brother thought it best to restrain the body. But as you have discerned, my mind and my tongue remain my own. Well, for the present at least. As for him," and he pointed at a pile of rags on a bench in the other corner, "my other esteemed sibling needs no restraining. In fact, I think he may even be dead already. At least he'll be warm where he's gone." Once more the brother's laugh grated on my agitated mind. "And he'll deserve every flame that Hades can serve up to him, no doubt. But I will say that it's very hard to find family loyalty these days." And at that, he spat on the floor in my direction.

I walked over towards the bench to see if indeed there was still any spark of life in the poor soul. I reached down and touched what I presumed was his brother's shoulder, and the wraith instantly sat up, his shrunken orbits staring wildly out at me from his skeletal face. Not a word did he utter. He had a terrified look as if he'd looked into Hell already and seen his doom. Then he flopped back down like a phantom and let out a long, lingering sigh.

"Forget him. He's just worthless fodder for the worms. What's your name?" the brother asked.

Thinking it a harmless thing to answer, I replied "Marco. And yours?"

"Giulio," he said, as if enjoying the sound of his name being spoken. "Giulio," he repeated. "My dear brother, the Duke, was threatened by my backside," and he laughed again. "Don't you get it? He was afraid my backside would sit on his ducal throne, so he decided to give me my very own kingdom down here, with rats for subjects. I hope you don't mind rats," he said, "because they're very busy in here when it gets dark." And he made scratching sounds with his long nails on the wall next to him. "And they have very sharp teeth, too." And again that piercing laugh echoed off the walls of his mad realm.

I do not know how many days I was in that forgotten place. There was never any real daylight, just enlightened gloom and sightless blackness. The only defining difference between the two was the sound of the rats scurrying around in the darkness, looking for any scraps of food that might have fallen from our plates where they were thrust under the doors of our living tomb.

I hadn't seen the jailer since he'd locked me away. All I'd heard was the sound of his feet scuffing along the flagstones outside and the jangle of the keys on his belt. Then one day our door creaked open, and the jailer went over to Giulio. He unlocked Giulio's chains from the wall, merely observing that there had been too much chat recently and that the instructions were for us to be separated. "But we were having so much fun," mocked Giulio. "But you're right. This idiot was completely boring. Not even the rats enjoyed his company," and with a parting spit, he left like a big child in chains. And I can thankfully say that I never saw nor heard of him again.

Shortly after that, the jailer returned. He went over to where Giulio's wretched brother lay and gave him a shove with his boot. "Been dead long?" he asked in a bored fashion.

"I didn't know that he was dead," I honestly replied. "But I'm certain he hasn't eaten anything for maybe a week."

"Get your clothes off," the jailer said.

"What?!" I answered uncomprehendingly.

He walked over to where I could see his face, and he repeated, "Get your clothes off. We ain't got much time." And as he spoke, that sense of recognition returned to me.

"What's going on?" I asked as I began to unbutton my tunic. The jailer was meanwhile struggling to remove the dead brother's clothing, too.

"Antonio's mi brother. Told me all about you. The lady . . . ," and here he indicated upwards with a jerk of his thumb, "she says to get you outta here pronto. So get your clothes off."

The understanding began to dawn in my consciousness, and I increased the speed of my undress.

"You swap places with 'im. They takes ya to the cemetery and bury you. Only Toni will be there to help you escape. Understand?" And he released each piece of information like the reluctant opening of a prison door.

"But what if Toni doesn't get there in time," I said, whilst pulling a foul-smelling shirt over my head. The jailer shrugged his shoulders and began to dress the body in my tunic.

"Not my problem," he replied philosophically. "'Urry up, they'll be 'ere to collect you soon." And even as he said the words, footsteps could be heard coming down the stone steps.

"Quick, 'elp me drag this bag o' bones over there an' we'll 'ide it under 'is Lordship's bench in the corner." The poor brother's remains were as light as a feather, the job swiftly completed. I had just enough time to lie down in the recently vacated spot and try to tame my breathing.

"Did yer bring the sack with yer?" enquired my friend the jailer.

A gruff voice grunted, "I 'opes as it's big enough," the voice said, "'e looks pretty big for a 'alf-starved beggar."

"That's 'cuz I take such good care of me prisoners," the jailer responded, which was met with leering laughter.

A musty sack was pulled down over my head and secured with rope below my feet.

"Probably best to drag 'im till we gets to the stairs, then we'll have to lump 'im up 'em between us," said the man with the gruff voice. They rolled me onto the floor, and it was all I could do not to cry out as my head hit the fractured flagstones. The journey up and out of the dungeon and onto the cart severely banged up my poor legs and arms, whilst my head throbbed at the repeated insults.

I was left in the cart for some time. Where it was located I had no idea, and so I had to remain as still as possible, even though my limbs screamed at me to move. For all I knew, I was in a courtyard surrounded by guards, so stillness was my only shield. Eventually, after much low chatter with unseen faces, the cart lurched forward, and we proceeded to the cemetery. Once there, I was again unceremoniously dumped on the ground, but this time onto softer soil that had the smell of being freshly turned. I was lying by my own grave, but there was no sound of Toni, and panic began to rise in my heart.

The sound of shoveling started next to me, and the sound of clay falling on clay hinted of imminent death. Cascades of fresh soil tumbled into a black, unseen depth, making the hairs on my neck rise and a light sweat break out on my brow.

"Looks deep enough to me," said a previously unheard voice. "Yers don't want to bury 'im standing up, do yers?" There was a scrambling of limbs and the sound of heavy breathing as the man climbed out of my grave.

"OK," he said, "give 'im the 'eave 'o," and with the bottom of his foot, the gravedigger's assistant pushed me into a living nightmare. "Where is Toni?" my brain screamed to me, "why hasn't he arrived by now?" Despite myself, I began to move just a little bit as the first shovelful of worm-laden earth landed on my covered head.

"Come on," said the gravedigger, "why don't yer give me an 'and, then we can get 'ome early. 'ow come it's always me what does the diggin'?"

"'Cos there's only one shovel, that's why," replied his assistant. And it was because of the simple fact that there was only one shovel that I lived to tell this tale. More earth was slowly filled in on top of me and soon breathing became more difficult under the heavy damp soil.

"Oy," a voice called out and the digging halted, "are you the gravedigger?" The joy that flooded my heart when I recognized Toni's voice was indescribable.

"'Course I'm the gravedigger. Who do you think I was then? The Virgin Mary? Who are you?"

"Been sent 'ere from the palace. They've got another one for you. Slipped in the dungeon and bust' his neck, poor blighter. Strange 'ow these things 'appen, eh?"

"Best finish off filling this 'ere 'ole. Buggalugs 'ere won't do it, will yer?" said the gravedigger to his companion. This was met with a healthy sniff followed by a well-rehearsed spit.

"Ain't my job, bruvver. I'm just the driver in this business," he said.

"Well, you'd better get a move-on with this one, 'cos the jailer don't like dead bodies in 'is dungeon. Says they make 'im feel creepy. Funny that, ain't it?" said Toni, who was obviously having a great time with his friends, whilst I slowly froze to death in that black, cold pit. "Why don't I finish off 'ere, and you clear off and fetch the uvver bloke. That ways everyone's a winner, and you owe me big time."

"Well, you just make sure you fill it in properly, OK? I've got standards, you know, and I've got a reputation to maintain, too." And I heard the sound of stamping feet as he stamped the clinging clay from his boots and listened to them as they faded from my hearing.

"Hang on," said Toni in a stage whisper, "they're almost gone." I tried to shout that I didn't have much choice, but the muddy sack that covered my face prevented any sound escaping.

I felt the thud of his boots landing on either side of me, and then his hands were scraping away the soil that covered me. A knife appeared before my face, and then a brilliant light blinded me. I drank the sweet air into my lungs, and its sweetness imprinted itself on my memory. How little we think of the air we breathe, those gentle evening breezes, the icy winds from wintered hills, those fierce gales lacerated with falling rain. Only a man who is gasping for life can fully understand what a gift it is to breathe great lungfuls of clean air.

Toni helped me struggle up from my living grave, pushed me back out over the rim, and restored me to life. Then after climbing out himself, we embraced like brothers. "We'd best finish the job," he said, "and leave it lookin' like it's a proper grave." And giving me one of his winks, he picked up the shovel and began his labor.

"Feels a bit odd, filling in your grave and you 'ere sitting next to me," he said with a cheeky grin.

"It feels wonderful to me," I said back, "Thank you, Toni. You've saved my life. And your brother, too. Tell him I will be eternally grateful to him."

"Well, you'll be the first customer of 'is to 'ave ever said that," said Toni, beavering away at the job. "If all goes to plan, then the real body should be in the ground in a few hours, and we should be a long ways off by then."

"I can't leave without Clare," I told him.

"I know," said Toni, pausing to gather his breath and leaning on his shovel. "That's exactly what the lady said: 'He won't leave without his little girl. But he won't 'ave to.' That's 'er exact words." And he wiped some sweat from his brow and returned to completing the grave. When he had finished the job, he stabbed the spade into the brown earth, spat on both hands and said, "Good riddance to bad rubbish," turned on his heels, and left. I followed Toni to where he'd left his horse tethered to a tree. There he unlaced a pack behind the saddle and handed it to me, saying, "The lady sent you this. She said you're to follow the road south until someone makes contact with you."

"But who's going to contact me, and what about Clare? Where is she?" I demanded of the poor fellow.

He looked at me with soft, humble eyes, scratched his head, and said simply, "Dunno."

"I'm sorry Toni. I didn't mean to shout, but after all the treachery we've been through, it gets difficult to believe these people sometimes."

"I knows how you feel, Marco," the quiet man said, "we poor people often feel let down by them what has the power over us. But this lady is different. Some say terrible things about what she's done in the past, but if you were to ask me, I'd say at 'eart she's a good woman. That's what she is, a good woman."

"And I trust you, Toni, though it tests my deepest fears to walk away from my little girl." And we again embraced like brothers, whilst the horse chewed on its bit behind us.

"You stink," said Toni, pushing me away with a grin. "You'd better change into them clothes that she sent, uv-verwise you'll be dead of the smell yourself before youse get to the next village."

When I untied the bundle, fresh clothes fell to the ground at my feet, and in their midst was a small packet.

I quickly tore off my rags, which Toni tied to a big rock and dropped in a nearby stream. The clothes I put on were clean workman's clothes which had been carefully chosen. I pushed the packet inside my shirt with the intention of opening it when I had time to myself later on.

"Well, bruvver," Toni said, "I'm off now. You take care, and if you see that little urchin Coppino, tell 'im I'll see 'im in Rome. And tell 'im 'e's a good lad, and that Toni said so." And after embracing each other once more, he mounted his horse and left. I watched that simple, honest man disappear out of sight.

I turned to head south and felt his absence immediately. When you leave the embrace of simple kindness laced with honest trust, you experience a diminishing of self, and I felt smaller because I had parted from that good man.

The road south was over flat terrain, and I covered the leagues quickly. After some hours, I sat under the shade of a tree and took the package from my jacket to open it. Inside there was a letter with some golden coins. And inside the letter was a small, neat square of silk. I opened it and discovered a beautiful golden crucifix with a fine gold chain. I held it in the palm of my callused hand and stared in awe at its beauty. Placing it back carefully inside the silken cloth, I put the folded square back inside my tunic and opened the letter. The scent that emanated from it immediately aroused vivid memories.

Dear Signor Marco,

I am sorry that I cannot be there with you to say a final farewell. Sometimes in life unexpected people cross your path: some for good, some for ill. Yet there are a rare few who reach into your heart and stay there forever. Thank you, Marco, for being such a person. Your wife is truly blessed to be married to such a man as you. The crucifix is my gift to your wife. It was mine once, but such gifts as it represents cannot be owned by one single person. In time, perhaps she will pass it on to the person who best deserves it.

Your daughter, and my blessed goddaughter, is an exceptional person. She is surely a gift from God. But He has given her a better father than her godmother could ever have offered her. I know you will always love and care for her, and I bless and thank you for that. I will try to do whatever I can to help her in the years ahead, but I fear that I may not be able to do much. Even a duchessa has a lord she must obey.

Marco, we shall never see each other this side of Paradise, but I thank you for the brief time we spent together, and I pray that one day we will all meet merrily in Heaven.

Your friend,

L

I read the letter several times before finally folding it and placing it next to the crucifix in my bosom. I sat there for several minutes remembering each detail of our brief encounter, and the intoxicating emotions it had created. "There but for the grace of God . . . ," I muttered to myself. Then I began to understand that Lucrezia was a captive of her circumstances—birth, power and wealth—and yet had managed to keep a sacred place in her heart for kindness and even love. Whilst poor, humble unknown me—well in the end, I was far richer than she would ever be in this world, in terms of loving and being loved. And touching my breast, I whispered to myself, "I will not forget you, my lady."

I looked up at the sound of a horse cantering down the road. "Toni," I cried in joyful surprise. And then with sudden fear in my heart, "Is there something wrong?"

Toni slowed to a halt and behind him sat my darling Clare. "Papa," she beamed as she slid from the saddle and rushed into my arms. "Oh Papa, I'm so glad to see you're safe and well. They didn't harm you, did they?"

Between the laughter and the tears, we hugged and shared our stories: even Toni joined in with how his brother had explained the unexpected accident of Marco and had left the poor gravediggers to explain why his body had been put in the local lime kiln and not buried in a pauper's grave. "We fought 'e 'ad the plague," was the story they told. Not a mention was made of the gold ducat in each of their pockets that had so convinced them of that story.

"And did the Lady treat you well?" I asked at last.

Clare gave me a quizzical look before saying "She was wonderful to me, Papa. Is it true that she's my real Mamma?"

"Yes, my precious," I replied, my hand holding hers, "she is. And in a different world, in a different time perhaps, I think she would have been a wonderful mother to you, too."

"Perhaps," she mused. "It's fun living in a palace for a few days," she said, "but they're really drafty and cold, and everyone seems to know your business." And tossing her head back, she added, "Anyway, I much prefer living with my real family. Sarah will never believe all the things that go on in such a place."

We both laughed at the thought of the two of them sharing their recent experiences. "I hope they're safe," I said. "I hope they meet someone as kind as our lady."

Clare looked coyly at me and said, "I think she really liked you, Papa." I felt my face heat up under her look before Toni broke in, saying "I 'spect His Lor'ship may not like you quite as much," and we all laughed out loud.

"I think the best thing for us to do now is to head back to Rome and see if we can get news of how Laura and the children are. Maybe the Dom or Julian will have some news by now," I said.

"From what I 'ear," said Toni, "Cesare Borgia is in a spot of bother and won't be heading home to Marche to be puttin' 'is feet up in the near future. So maybe there's some 'ope to be found there, eh?"

"Well, we've some days' travel in front of us, so we'd best make a move. We can pick up some fresh horses in the next town with the money the lady gave me."

"And she gave me some, too," said Clare, tapping her belt.

"Me, too," said Toni, tapping the hat on his head. "Who'd a thought of stealing a poor fellow's 'at. Boots is a different thing. Lotsa people don't 'ave boots. But 'ats . . . ," and he made a sweeping bow which made us both laugh. "I may not be the sharpest sword in a scabbard, but when it comes to gold, I keeps that sort o' information under mi 'at."

Dom

TAKES UP HIS
STORY AGAIN

THE FOUR MEN had listened to me for some time now. They appeared to be good and kindly men, and the flickering fire was mirrored in each of their bearded faces. Niccolo was the first to speak, whilst the wind howled around the house like a wolf, sending icy drafts through the loose-fitting windows and doors.

"Life can be a strange journey," he said, and his eyes gleamed with enthusiasm. "We've been on a journey of sorts, too, Dom," and looking around at his friends as if seeking their permission, he continued, "Our families were once Cathars. It's not a pretty story to tell. Our ancestors were French way back when, but were hunted from their homes like animals just because they had a different view of God. I suppose you've heard of the Inquisition?" He gave a shrug and tapped the side of his head. "Sometimes the human race seems completely mad."

"We also heard of this Englishman of yours and were on our way to listen to him when we found you the other day. It's taken us weeks to travel through the passes around here, because only a crazy person would travel at this time of year." And he smiled at his friends, saying, "Welcome to the madhouse! But my point is that if there had been any pilgrim monk on the road, then we would have heard of him. As you may have gathered, there aren't that many ways to cross a mountain when winter storms are raging!"

"Are you sure?" I asked in ignorance. Carlo pulled a glove off his hand and held it in front of my face.

"Those fingers weren't black three weeks ago. Take a close look, friend. Frostbite. If your Rosso tried any other path than the one we were on, he'd be a frozen corpse by now." Then he carefully put the glove back on his frost-bitten hand.

"So you think that Rosso is still in Italy?"

"If the Englishman is as holy as you say, then your Rosso is probably still sitting under an olive tree and saying his prayers in the warm sunshine," said Carlo with a grin. "But why are you up here having swimming lessons in Lake Como when Siena is even closer to Rome than Florence is?"

"That's a very good question," I replied sheepishly, "and I have a very simple answer. I thought I was being smart, but by all appearances I've been pretty stupid. But let me put you more in the picture.

"When Pietro came back and told us about Marco, Laura, and their family being kidnapped, we were totally confused by what was going on. Then Pietro told us of his little street urchins who'd been following the carts that had abducted Marco and the family. We came to the conclusion that it must have been something to do with Clare, and that it was somehow linked to what Cardinal Ville-prieux had said to Rosso. Seeing as how Rosso was the only one who really knew what had happened in Paris, we assumed that he had his own idea as to who Clare's Mamma really was. So it was vital that someone go off and find him. Then little Coppino, he's one of Pietro's little helpers, returned and told us how he'd climbed on the back of one of the coaches up at Monte Sacro, close by where the kidnapped family had been taken.

"Somewhere along the way, hunger had met tiredness and he'd fallen asleep. Then suddenly he was discovered, and he thought his end had come--but Marco, the black-smith who was with Clare, had stepped in and saved him. Whilst Coppino was getting a meal at the coach stop, he managed to tell everything he knew to Clare, and she told him that it appeared that they were being taken to Ferrara. The mystery of her mother seemed more unreal than any of us had anticipated. Clare said that they were headed to the D'Este palazzo in Ferrara.

"Knowing this, we all thought it was really important that we get a message to Rosso. The only lead we had there was Brother William in Siena, so we decided that seeing as I was the only one who was really free to travel, that I should go and look for Rosso. Perhaps it might have been better if they'd chosen someone with a few more brains between his ears!

"I traveled light and had a few coins in my pocket to keep me fed and dry along the way. The dawn starts were the hardest, with that damp cold seeping into every joint and muscle. But when that sun sent blues and oranges throughout the morning mist over the countryside, well, it did my heart good to be out on the road again. Getting to Siena isn't difficult, just one foot in front of the other and a big dash of persistence and you're there. The only problem was that I couldn't actually travel to where Brother William was, as there was a little war going on in that area, and neither side wanted any outsiders spying on what they were doing. And that included one-eyed, one-armed men looking for English mystics! Some people have very suspicious minds, eh?" And again the group chuckled in agreement.

"So I headed out around the western side of Siena hoping to creep in from the north. The countryside in that part of the world is beautiful, even in winter, but soon some landmarks reminded me of the last time I had been there: bitter memories of a brutal battle. I then remembered that Rosso's Agnes lived somewhere in that area, and it came to me that perhaps I should seek her out, just in case he had called past there himself.

"As Rosso had told us, it was difficult to find her house. It's in such an out-of-the-way place, but I asked at some of the farmhouses, and they didn't seem to be threatened too much by the looks of me. Some even invited me in to rest and gave me a feed. Good folk. Good-hearted folk.

"So eventually I found myself walking down a winding path not far from the river where Agnes had dragged Rosso back into this world. The nearby cottage was neat and homey, and deep in my heart I felt I'd always known the place, even though it was just like so many of the other isolated cottages that dotted the landscape. I knocked at the door, half-expecting that it'd be empty and that I'd wasted precious days searching for something that was no longer there. But the door opened, and a young man stood there looking at me like he'd seen a ghost!

"'What do you want?' he spat out at me.

"Sometimes, being much bigger than other people does have certain advantages," and the others nodded in smirking agreement.

"'That's a fine way to greet a stranger,' I said to him. The man's close-set eyes darted looks behind me to see if there was anyone else with me.

"'You have to be careful, sir. There are some willful men abroad and not all can be trusted.' And with that, he stepped outside the door and closed it behind him. 'How can I help you?'

"'Some information would be nice,' I said to him, and I rubbed my beard with this stump of mine just to annoy him with its ugliness. 'Who are you will do for a start,' I said, leaning down over him.

"'I'm Fredo, and this is my home,' was his reply, but every fiber of my mind knew he was lying through his teeth.

"'That's strange,' I said, 'I thought Agnes owned this farm.'

"'Well, that's sort of true,' he replied, 'she's my wife.'

"'Your wife?' says I.

"'Yes, Signore,' he replied, and taking hold of my arm started to lead me away from the door. His grip felt weak, and his palm was damp with sweat, which made me pull my arm away. 'I feel we got off on the wrong foot,' he said, trying to gain my confidence. 'My wife has been ill, and it's best that we don't disturb her. Now, what would you like to know?'

"'Your wife'—and the very word stuck in my throat as I said it, 'once knew a man called Rosso, and I was wondering whether he'd called past here recently. It's very important that I know, 'cos I've got a very important message for him, and the sooner I'm on my way, the better for both of us,' I said. And this time it was me gripping his arm, which made him flinch with the power of it.

"'Rosso, you say,' he said. 'I've heard my wife speak of him, but no, he hasn't been through these parts.' And from the look on his face, I thought that he was telling the truth.

"'Have you heard of an Englishman called Brother William, then?' I asked him.

"'Oh yes,' he said, and he couldn't stop his eyes from darting back to the door of the house.

"'Something bothering you, friend?' I asked him.

"'No, nothing. I just hope that the dear woman is resting well.' And he fashioned a half smile on those smooth, shifty features of his. 'Brother William I can help you with. Agnes often talks of him. She's a very devoted lady, my wife. Anyway, he's been living on the other side of Siena for some time, but I heard recently that he's gone back to England.' And even as he said it, I knew that he was lying. But it planted a small seed of doubt in my mind, and I knew he could see it.

"'Sorry I can't help you anymore. I would ask you in, but with my wife the way she is . . . ,' and he shrugged his shoulders and smiled patronizingly at me. I had a great urge to flatten him there and then.

"'If I find that you've been lying to me, then these here knuckles of mine are going to have a field day with your face,' I said to him. But he turned his back, closed the door behind him and left me standing alone on the stone path, uncertain as to whether to knock the door down or leave him alone.

"I muttered an oath under my breath and thought to myself that not everything he told me could have been lies. So I decided to take a chance and believe him. I turned back to the highway and headed for Florence. My plan was to go from there on up to Milan, where I thought I might get some more information. I got to San Gimiano and hired a horse. He was a tired and scrawny beast, but as my journey went on, he seemed to get stronger and stronger. By the time I got to Milan, I was sad to leave him behind. And I think he was sad to see the back of me, too.

"He would have been sadder if you'd tried to make him swim across the lake," said Cristofero, and the others laughed with him.

"I shall ignore that comment, Cristofero," I said, smiling along with them, "but one good thing I did do before I left San Gimiano was to send a message to Gino. He and Maria lived not far away from there, and I thought he might have heard something of Rosso. If nothing else happened, it was good to think that he'd be thinking of us, just like old times. Anyway, I went bumbling along up to Milan asking if anyone had heard of the Englishman. Some said they had, but most had never heard of him. But no one could tell me where he was."

"I had to make a decision: turn back to Siena and accept that I'd made the wrong choice, or head up to the border and see if I could pick up his trail there. But as you now know, I made the wrong decision and almost ended up as fish bait in Lake Como, which is where my story began."

There was a silence in the room as my companions digested all they'd heard.

Niccolo broke the silence. "I think we've heard all we need to hear. Brothers," he said, and we all looked at his gleaming face, "when this storm finally stops, we'll head down to Siena. There, God willing, I expect we'll find Brother William. And it's my belief that Dom will find his friend Brother Rosso sitting with him, in glorious solitude and making better sense of this world than we have so far."

Gino's
STORY

THE BLEATING OF the sheep woke me early even though it was still dark outside. The dark light of a winter morning has never been my best time, but hearing that bleat made me think immediately of a hungry fox or dog looking for an easy meal. I slipped out of the warm cocoon that was our bed and left Maria deeply asleep, enjoying a joyous respite from work and motherhood.

I shivered almost as a reflex as I pulled a thick sweater over my head and stood for a moment by the cot of our dear little daughter. Although I couldn't see her clearly, I knew she'd be lying flat on her back, arms flung out wide above her head, and her smooth face would crease with serene smiles. Maria had told me that when babies are growing in their mother's womb, God tells them all the secrets of the universe. And in those first few months of life, they slowly forget what He's told them. It's those fleeting memories that cause infants to smile so gloriously.

But the cold drove me to look for my trousers and to seek another pullover, too. Standing on one leg, I over-balanced in the dark and stumbled against the bed. Maria stirred, and I held my breath. She'd been up with little Bella during the cold, dark night and I knew she needed the extra sleep, so I froze with one naked leg half-raised. Not until her breathing resumed its deep, slow rhythm, and I knew she was still asleep, did I finish dressing.

Creeping out the door, I carefully closed the latch. I knew every board that creaked, so after walking over the bare floor like a child avoiding cracks on pavement, I made it into the kitchen without making a noise. I lit a lamp and shadows danced behind empty mugs and into the corners. I put some fuel on the damped-down fire and watched the glowing embers leap to life and send eddies of heat out into the room.

I grabbed a coat from behind the door and stepped out into the frosty night. Stars glittered like fire in the cold, clear sky. The moon was long gone below the horizon, and the sky was a marvel of twinkling delight. A sheep bleated again, then another, and I moved toward the pen where they were secured. I picked up my stick and gripped the icy wood in my bare hand. I reached into my pocket and found dry gloves there. I smiled because I knew I hadn't left them there. Maria always seemed to be thinking one step ahead of me. I half-turned and blew a kiss back in the direction of the house.

It was very dark outside, but there was a rim of crimson forming along the distant horizon that suggested the weather might be changing. I checked the sheep and the pen around them and all seemed secure. I checked the barn, and the door was closed tight. I stood in the middle of the yard breathing dragon's breath in the frosty air and listened. I heard a bird sing, its crystal sound piercing that dark moment with a note of the new day's hope. I turned and went back into the warm kitchen.

"It's a bit cold for a walk, my love." Maria was there at the stove, warming some soup left over from the day before and tearing a large chunk of bread from yesterday's loaf.

"What are you doing up, dearest?" I said, "I thought I'd crept out as silently as a mouse."

Smiling back at me, she said, "You did, best of all husbands, but I think Bella's hearing is better than mine-- and when she wakes up, she wants everyone else to join her!" And with that she walked towards me with our little bundle of love tucked snugly inside her shawl. Bella was feeding from Maria's full breast and making deliciously contented sounds as she did so.

"She's beautiful," I said, and we both just stood and stared in awe at our precious daughter as she stripped the milk from her mother's breast. "It's amazing. How does she know how to do all these things?" And I looked up at Maria in bemused wonder.

"It's because she's a girl. They're much smarter than boys, you know!" Our eyes locked, then we both burst out loud with laughter.

"It's a miracle," I said. "That's all I can say. It's a miracle."

"So why were you outside when it's so freezing cold?" Maria asked.

"There was something worrying the sheep, and I was checking it wasn't a fox or a stray pack of dogs. Some of the ewes are with lamb and being frightened by a pack of dogs could make them lose their babies." And looking at our little Bella, I said, "And I couldn't bear the thought of that, even for a sheep!"

We sat and broke our fast in the slowly lightening kitchen, enjoying the warmth that flowed out from the fire. The sheep began to stir again, which worried me.

"I'm going outside to check again," I said to Maria, pulling on my coat once more, but feeling a warm glow from the food in my belly. "Just in case." Stepping out into the bright light of a late winter's dawn, I saw that the eastern sky was full of heavy clouds, whilst overhead the sky was clear and blue. "Looks like more rain," I mumbled to myself and headed across the yard to the barn.

Pulling open the door and letting it swing with a bang against the wall, I entered the looming space. The air was laced with the sweet smell of last year's hay and the less delightful odor of fresh dung from the two milk cows.

The daylight sought out all the corners and reached into the hayloft where freshly muddied rungs on the loft ladder caught my attention. "That's new," I said under my breath and slowly mounted the steps. Lifting my head above the bales that I'd neatly stored there, I looked around. Nothing. Pulling myself onto the wooden floor, I slowly began to search the area. Some muddy footprints led to a small pile of loose hay between two bales. Taking a step back, I said in a loud voice, "OK, you can come out now," and waited silently for movement.

After a few seconds, the hay reared up and revealed a ragged youth of uncertain age with black hair that had never seen a comb, sunken eyes as black as coal, and a pinched face that hadn't been fed for some days. He shivered uncontrollably.

"When did you last eat?" I asked him sternly, but my heart was moved at the sight of his condition. He shrugged his shoulders, shivered, and wiped his tattered sleeve across his face to hide the first hint of a tear. "Come on, then. Follow me," I said and retreated down the ladder. I waited at the bottom, and eventually there was a scuffling of reluctant feet, soon followed by the sight of long, skinny legs. "This way," I indicated and headed off across the yard after securing the barn door. In the middle of the yard I paused, "Are there any more of you in there?" But the shake of his bedraggled head told me that he was all alone.

"Another one for breakfast, Maria," I called as we arrived at the kitchen. Maria appeared, Bella in arms, to see who had arrived at this early hour. "Found him up in the hayloft freezing," I said. "I don't reckon he could have eaten anything for a few days."

"Come here, boy, and sit by the fire," said Maria, beginning to bustle around the room and placing little Bella in my arms. The lanky youth—for such he was—shuffled toward the fire and sat in the corner soaking up the heat. I was distracted by little Bella, who'd taken a sudden interest in my nose and was gripping it and giggling at the same time. The youth had been watching her antics, and his face broadened into a wide smile.

Maria turned and placed a bowl of steaming soup and a big hunk of bread into his lap, saying "Go on, eat up. It'll do you good." With motherly love she plucked Bella from my arms and said, "She hasn't finished feeding. I'll go into the other room and leave you two men to talk." I stooped down and gave her a kiss on each cheek and one for little Bella, too. The famished youth had watched every move we'd made as he loaded every morsel from the bowl to his empty stomach.

"'E said you'd be good ta me," the youth said between spoonfuls of broth, wiping his lips with his hands, then licking them for good measure. And all the while his eyes searched the kitchen, taking it all in.

"Who said we'd be good to you?" I asked him. Although compassion may rule in our home, I'd lived on the road for too long to trust everything at face value. The haunted face in front of me with its darting eyes did not inspire much trust.

"The one-armed bloke with the patch over 'is eye," he responded between slurps of soup.

"Name of the one-armed man?" I retorted, leaning back against the wall behind me and folding my arms.

"Said you'd know the name Rosso, but that warn't 'is name, though." This was said as he wiped his bowl clean with the remnants of the bread. The name of Rosso made my heart jump from surprise, and I tried to hide it as much as I could. But the lad was sharp-eyed.

"So if yer know Rosso, then that makes you Gino. Right?" And a sly confidence grew in his face.

I pushed myself away from the wall and came and stood in front of him.

"You seem to know a lot of things, young lad, so tell me what the name of the man who sent you was, and what does he want with me?"

"Depends," he said examining the bowl for any tell-tale remnants. "'E said you might 'elp by a bit o' grease in mi palm."

"Name," I repeated and hoped that my voice had an edge of menace, "or it might be more than grease you get, young fella."

"OK, OK," he said, realizing that he might have tried to push his luck too far. "'E said 'is name was the Dom. Mean anyfing to yer?"

I stood there for a moment or two, then reached into my pocket for any spare coins that might be there and handed them over to him. "Here," I said, "an honest answer deserves a fair reward. What name do you go by?"

"Rabbit," he answered. "It's 'cos I run everywhere and keep disappearing down 'oles," and he smiled a genuine smile that made us both relax a little. "Mi real name is Paolo, but no one ever calls me that. Which is a good thing, 'cos I don't like it much. Mi ole lady called me that. Said it was mi ole man's name, too, but seeing as I never met 'im, I 'ad to take that on trust—she weren't the most 'onest woman I ever knew."

"I need to know more about this man who calls himself the Dom, and why did he send you here?"

"Big fella, eh? Kind, too. He'd heard about mi from some fella and gave mi a meal and a few coins to come and give yer a message. Trouble is, I got done over on the way 'ere and was robbed of mi money. Seeing as it was easier to come 'ere than go back, I came on 'ere. 'e said you an' 'im was mates, and the free of youse did a lot a traveling togevver. 'E said that this Rosso was some sort of monk now and was somewhere near Siena, but that 'is little girl was in real trouble, and 'e needed your 'elp."

"Little girl? Do you mean Clare?" I asked.

"Dunno 'er name, Gino. But someone's taken 'er and 'er family, and your Dom wanted to get a message to Rosso, 'cos 'e thought that this Rosso'd know who might a dunnit. Summink about a Englishman called Brother

William. Never 'eard of 'im miself, but then I'm not in that line of business, eh?" And again he smiled an endearing, boyish smile. Then his face fell and took on a more feral look. "But there's some not so good news, too, Gino. Your Dom also finks that this young girl 'as been taken to Ferrara to the palazzo of the Duke D'Este, and the word is that 'e 'as the most grumpy dis-per-zition of all the dukes in this part of the world."

"D'Este," I muttered to myself.

"He's the one who married that Lucrezia lady. You know, the one who's supposed to be the pope's daughter," said my beloved Maria, reentering the room with both arms free. "Bella's fast asleep. It's amazing what a good meal does for an empty stomach," she said with a smile.

"Tell me about it," said Rabbit with a grin.

"Did Dom say what he was going to do next?" I asked my now very happy and content guest.

"'E said to tell yer that 'e'd 'ead up norf to cut your Rosso off. But if 'e didn't find 'im up there, 'e might at least get some news of 'im along the way. Then if 'e 'adn't got any news by then, 'e'd backtrack down towards Siena. If you asks me, it sounded a pretty daft idea, but then 'e was a bit bigger than me an' who am I to argue under such circusstarnces?"

So much news had arrived in our peaceful kitchen that my head spun with it all.

"I'll get some wood for the fire," I said to Maria. "It'll help clear my spinning head and give me time to work out what it all means.

"Need a 'and?" asked Rabbit. "First time I've been outta town fer ever such a long time. "'ave you got chick-ins, too? I love chick-ins. We 'ad sum when I was a lad growing up . . ."

"Perhaps you'd better stay here with me, my lad," said Maria with her firm voice. It was the one she reserved for me when one of my ideas was a little more ridiculous than normal. "You've got a year's worth of grime behind your ears, so a good wash won't do you any harm. And I think some of Gino's old clothes might keep you a bit warmer than those threadbare rags you're wearing."

"I ain't dirty," Rabbit responded in a hurt voice, but even he cowered when my gentle little lady gave him one of her looks! "S'pose it won't do any 'arm," he was saying, as I went out into the cold daylight.

The clouds on the horizon had approached and were pushing the clear, blue sky back into a thin band behind the hills. The air felt warmer, though a breeze would soon spring up, and with the threatened rain, the damp air would soon feel colder than a frost. I hurried to the woodpile behind the shed. The cattle and sheep needed feeding and so did the chickens, but I thought I'd get Rabbit to feed them later and check for eggs, once he'd been scoured by the lady of the house.

My heart was lightened to hear the names of the Dom and Rosso after such a long time. Great memories came back to me of all our times on the road together. But I wondered what had become of that Frenchman Ville-prieux? There had been no mention of him. Perhaps he'd gone back to France? Too bad, really, but I was glad that he wasn't mentioned in the same breath as the other two. He was likeable enough, but he was different from us. He was both flamboyant and secretive, tough yet tender, happy and melancholic too. It would be unfair to blame all that on him being French—then again, it could explain a lot of things!

But Rosso a monk! I didn't see that coming. Falling in love, perhaps. He always carried his heart on his sleeve, and I always took him for the marrying kind. And the Dom? Rabbit had said, "One arm, one eye."

How did that happen? How had Dom managed to survive like that? Who had been looking after him? And who would have done that to one of the most gentle creatures the good Lord ever created?

My thinking was no clearer as I pulled dry wood from the stack and rummaged around for some dry kindling, too. I reached for the hatchet to make sure that we'd have enough dry kindling for the next few days, just in case that rain set in for longer than usual. Thinking about poor Dom's injuries caused a small fury in my brain, and I buried the hatchet in the stump whilst the kindling shot off in two different directions. "Steady, lad," I said to myself, "more brains, less brawn."

A few minutes later, I was backing in through the kitchen door with my arms full of wood, and I dropped the load by the fire. Rabbit sat in a miasma of steam as Maria scrubbed parts of his neck that had been almost tattooed with grim. "Your dear wife," Rabbit said without looking up, "has a pretty wicious streak in her, Gino."

"Less of that cheek or I'll really put some effort into it," retorted Maria with a motherly smile.

"A scene of domestic bliss." I smiled back at them both.

"I'm not sure about the bliss bit, Gino," Rabbit said, which was met with a light flick of the towel from Maria.

"Less of your cheek, my son," she said. "Have you had any thought about what to do, Gino?" she said, looking straight at me.

"I have, my dear. If Dom needs our help, then he must get it. And seeing as he's gone up to the northwest, I think I should head to Ferrara to see if I can pick up the girl's trail from there. At least then I can return back down the path from there to Siena and hopefully catch up with the Dom in that area. What do you think?"

"I must admit that I don't like the idea of being here alone with the cattle to look after with no man in the house. Before you came back, at least I always had the comfort of knowing that Papa was in the house, but with him gone this twelve months now, it'll be very strange without either of you. But I agree. You have to do something and I can't think of a better plan, so be off with you."

"Hold on, Maria. I haven't finished yet. It's come to my attention that this young lad seems to be very fond of chickens," I said, moving to stand close to the young man, "aren't you, Rabbit?"

"Maybe," he replied, whilst developing a nervous tic around his left eye. "Why?"

"Well, as the saying goes 'Better an egg today than a chicken tomorrow.' So, Rabbit stays here till I get back. He helps around the farm. He gets his food and board and you, Maria, have your security. Then when I get back we can decide what to do."

"I ain't 'spected to 'ave to change the baby's diapers, am I?" asked Rabbit with a shocked expression, glancing first at me and then at Maria.

"If you stay here, my lad, you'll do what I tell you to do!" said Maria, folding her arms in that imperious attitude designed to subdue any attempt at male dominance.

"I have no doubt that the two of you will get on really well. But first I need to show Rabbit the ropes. Come on, Maria can teach you about the diapers later." And winking at Maria, the complaining Rabbit and I put on some coats and went outside.

I left the following day for Ferrara. I didn't have much to go on, apart from the fact that the Lady Lucrezia would have recently received a young girl into her household. Then there was the reputation of her husband. Grumpy didn't really cover the maliciousness of the man. He was reported to have had his brothers thrown into prison on the pretext that they were after his estates. But at least he had stood up to that unpleasant brother of Lucrezia's— now he was really a piece of work!

It took me almost a week to travel from the farm to Ferrara. The weather was terrible and the roads heavy with mud. The mountains we crossed were capped with snow, and the icy rain stung my face like fierce flint flakes. Fellow travelers were few and far between. My tired legs were treated to the occasional respite by the kindness of tradesmen moving by cart between Florence and Bologna. But the days were long and wet, and the nights cold and damp. By the time I had crossed the flat fields of Ferrara, not even my dear Maria would have recognized the mud-splattered person who entered the gates, seeking out a hostel where he could find a hot bath and a change of clothes.

Few things are more enjoyable than stripping off cold, clinging clothes and stepping into a hot bath in front of a warm fire. My numb toes went through stages of intense agony. But slowly the heat percolated throughout my whole body, and I slumped lower and lower into that sublime heat.

Climbing out of that bath took great determination, but I didn't dare stray too far from the warmth of the fire. Tiptoeing around the steaming pile of muddy vestments that were once clothes, I reached out for the warm ones I'd purchased on my arrival. Soon I was warm, clean, and dry—the holy trinity of the tired traveler. Only one thing remained: food. This was soon ordered and eaten with relish, and I slumped back on the bed a very happy man. I must have dozed because when I awakened, it was already dark outside and the rain was hitting the window with great determination, driven on by the wild wind. I went down to the taverna to join the throng that had gathered at day's end.

Strangers always evoke questions, and soon I was engaged by the keeper of the taverna as we began to barter information. Soon he knew that I was a down-on-his-luck farmer from near Siena, traveling the land looking for work. I had discovered that a young girl and her father had recently arrived as guests of the duchessa, but no one had seen either of them since their arrival a few weeks back. When I returned to my room a little later, I turned this information over in my mind. The presence of a "father" confused me, but otherwise the facts fitted well with the story given me by Rabbit. I determined that the next morning I would go to the palazzo and see if I could find the people who had brought the pair here and perhaps learn more from them. But first a good night's sleep called, and my body gratefully complied.

I awoke to a brilliantly clear morning. A sharp frost filtered the air so that each breath was like the first breath ever taken. The cold air cleansed the skin on my face like an icy washcloth, and the grass crackled under my warm, dry boots, which made me smile. When I arrived at the gates of the grand palazzo, I was challenged by the guard. I told him I was a farmer looking for work.

"Join the queue, my friend," was his dispassionate reply. "Unless you're prepared to shovel manure, there's not much use for farmers here." And with that, he pushed me in the chest as if to dismiss me.

Some things really annoy me. Perhaps it was just the delayed tiredness after a long journey. Perhaps it was worry about how Maria and the baby were faring with Rabbit, or perhaps it was just because this man was a bully who loved pushing people around that touched a sore nerve. But when the man's hand touched my chest, I felt my whole body turn into a granite rock that wasn't going to budge one tiny inch. My eyes burned with anger as I whispered with barely controlled rage, "Are you trying to tell me something, soldier? Or do I need to ask someone else about getting a job here?"

His eyes widened, and he shrank back. His uniform and helmet must have suddenly felt several sizes too large for his adolescent frame.

"Look," he muttered, looking quickly around him, "I'm just doing my job, master. No need to take it out on me. If it's a job you're looking for, then try the stables around back." He stepped aside to let me through. "And ask for Toni," he shouted after me. "He's a farmer, too."

"Thanks," I said, smoothing down the front of my jacket and locking my temper back where it belonged.

Climbing up the slope past the thick walls at the base of the palazzo, I followed the horse droppings until I came to the stables. "Anyone here seen Toni?" I shouted into the gloom.

"Over here," came a voice from one of the stalls. The handle of a rake appeared, which was soon followed by an unremarkable head with a simple smile and a small scar on one cheek. "Well, what can I do for you today, my friend?"

"Salve, friend. Any chance of a job—any job—for a poor farmer down on his luck?"

"You must be the third person this week who's asked me that, but sorry, friend, it's not up to me. You'd have to ask my caporale, but he's a prickly one at the best of times. I'll tell you what, though, this may be your lucky day! I may have to, er, go on leave soon, and they'll be needing someone to cover for me when I'm away. An' you look like a bloke who wouldn't shy away from a bit of hardship," he said, stroking the small scar on his cheek. "And believe me, 'ardship is the caporale's second name!" And saying that, he stabbed his pitchfork into a pile of manure nearby.

"Wait 'ere, I'll be back in a mo' . . . ," and with that, he put on his jacket and went out of the stable, leaving me alone with the horses. They were fine-looking beasts and obviously well cared for. I walked over to a large bay and patted him on the neck.

"Okay, boy," I said in his ear, "Now what stories can you tell me about what goes on here?"

"Like stories, do you?" boomed a voice from the door. "Telling people how to shovel shit is my favorite." Looking up, I saw the large figure of a man, with the smaller figure of his underling waving his arms at me from behind his caporale's back. From the underling's wild semaphores, I guessed that he wanted me to listen more than speak.

"Whatever you say, Caporale," I responded, in as meek a tone as I could muster.

"I like this man," the caporale said turning to his underling and swiping him across the top of his head, "but I'll miss seeing that smiling face of yours up to your ears in horse manure. Still," he said putting his powerful arm around the poor man's shoulders and giving him a rib-cracking squeeze, "you're much better at guarding than working, eh? Sitting on your backside watching prisoners comes far more natural to the likes of you and your mob, don't it?" Ducking away from the ensuing swipe at his head, Toni replied "Yes, Caporale. Whatever you say, Caporale," and he hurried over to where I was standing on the other side of the horse stall.

"OK, my fine fella. You fill the new man in on what needs to be done here and then report to the duchessa after you've washed, 'cos you stink of shit," the big man sneered at him. "Dunno why she's taken a shine to a weasel rat like you. It can't be nothing to do with your looks or your intelligence. Perhaps it's something you're hiding from me," he said, and his lecherous grin revealed several foul teeth to match his foul talk.

"It's 'cos I'm good with kids, that's all, Caporale," Toni said, shuffling his feet in the straw.

"Well, you'd better be gone before I gets back, or there'll be hell to pay." And saying that, he checked both his boots for any clinging reminder of the stables and left.

"He's a friendly sort," I said to Toni with a smile.

"Yes," he replied rubbing the scar on his cheek. "We two've been really intimate wiv each other. 'e give me this a few weeks back, just 'cos I was kind to a coupl'a people we was bringing to see her ladyship."

"Oh yes?" I asked trying to sound as offhand as I could, but my heart was beginning to gallop inside my chest. But Toni remained mute. "Pick people up often then, do you?" I nudged him in a friendly tone.

"It's mi job ain't it? Picking people up. That's what guards do, see?" and he chuckled to himself at his own little joke.

"Local people, or can you just pick up anyone, say like Romans or Venetians?"

"These last two was Romans. A man and 'is daughter. Nice bloke. He stepped in front of me when Boof 'ead tried to whip me again." Once again the fingers explored the redness of the still-healing scar. "but Marco—that was 'is name—he caught the end of it an' pulled 'im off his perch. I tell you what, Boof'ead warn't too 'appy when 'e got outta the dust, but that Marco stared 'im down and 'e didn't try it anymore."

"So what happened to Marco and his daughter then?" I continued trying to sound as casual as I could whilst picking up the hay fork and moving some dung into a pile.

Toni began to look decidedly uncomfortable and said, "I think I've said too much already friend. Me and my big mouth. I'd better show you what's gotta be done 'ere or else Caporale might just decide to take the whip to the both of us. Come on." And with that he walked me around and showed me what chores were in store for me. Most husbanding stables are the same: fodder, water, check the tackle, and clean out the manure. The rounds of the barn were soon complete, and Toni made to leave.

"Don't forget to wash, Toni," I said. "And maybe a change of clothes might be a good idea, too," I added, pointing to the splashes of mud on his trousers.

"Thanks, friend. But I'll be needing this kit pretty soon if the duchessa has her way," and a knowing look lingered over the strange smile that flickered around his lips. "Wish I could 'ang around. But you know what it's like with the ladies, eh?" and bowing low, he left.

I began thinking about all that had been said. It seemed that Clare and her father were here and that his name was Marco, a name I hadn't heard of before. Still, if Clare had someone good and kind with her, that could only be a good thing. But then Toni seemed to be acting in a strange way. Why the act about the lady, and what was that all about with the need for dirty clothes? I came to the conclusion that I needed to know more about Toni and hopefully gain his confidence. If I was lucky, then that should lead me to Clare, and I could work out what to do next.

"Lovely smell, ain't it?" Those mocking words could only have been said by one person, and so without looking up I said, "I prefer the smell of a pretty lady myself, Caporale. But each to his own taste." To my detriment, I quickly learned that the caporale liked to be the only co-median on the stage and felt the full force of his boot on my backside, causing me to fall headlong into a steam-ing pile of manure.

"The only female you're going to get close to my son is a mare. Where's that idle sod Toni gone to? 'As he slipped away already to the duchessa? That bloke wouldn't know 'ard work if it came up and bit 'im on the bum." And he folded his arms across his chest and leaned against the door of the stall. "So tell me Mister Farmer, what's the real reason you're 'ere?"

"Told you already, Caporale. A man's got to live. And he can't feed his family when some idiot in a silk cloak decides he don't like the look of you, but has an eye on your missus and decides to kick you off your land and steal your woman." Perhaps there was something that resonated in the caporale's mind, for he seemed to soften a little.

"Yeah," he muttered, "the bastards can be cruel sometimes."

Changing the subject quickly so that he didn't follow up with any more questions, I asked him where Toni was from. "That idle son of a bitch. Comes from a large family near 'ere. Brother's the jailer. Just like him. 'appy to sit on 'is backside all day and watch 'em dig ditches and cess-pools during the day, before 'e chains 'em back up on the cell walls at night." He cracked an evil smiled which sent shivers down my back. "'E lives somewhere on the other side of the piazza near the Church. Why do you ask?"

"He asked me for a loan and I gave him my last coin, so I need to get it back, otherwise I might have to eat the horses' rations." The caporale laughed.

"I reckon you've seen the last of that friend."

"Still. I want to get it back. Do you have his address?" He told me where Toni lived and left. I watched him go and thought that even though he was a tough, malig-nant man, there was still something good inside of him. I prayed that others saw it, too.

A few days later, I was lying in my straw-filled cot above the horse stalls thinking that God must be a very happy person. Watching us humans rushing about making our plans, thinking that we've got it all worked out, would be enough to bring a smile to the most mis-erable of gods. The reason I was lying in my cot in the first place was because I'd suddenly come down with a fever, which had made me feel like my arms and legs were made of lead and my strength that of a two-year-old. Sweat coursed down my back every time a paroxysm of coughing racked my aching body, and my head felt like the inside of a blacksmith's fire. By all accounts, hundreds of locals had come down with the fever, but few appeared to have been fatally afflicted, which I suppose was mildly reassuring.

But even though I felt as useless as a wet rag, I still had to look after the horses, and at least they appeared to be more understanding of me than the caporale! He seemed to delight in everyone's weaknesses and frequently lacerated us all with his comments or his whip. I struggled to my feet and descended via the ladder to the back of the barn. I had just picked up some oats to fill the horse troughs when my avenging angel stormed through the door. He was incandescent with rage, shouting "Where is that weaselly little bastard?"

Propping myself against the stall whilst wiping the sweat from my face, I foolishly asked "Who's that, Caporale?" This was met with the full force of his fist in the middle of my chest which knocked all the wind from my lungs and dropped me like a sack of turnips.

"That rat Toni, you fool. He's been trying to hide something from me for weeks," he yelled, kicking the trough I'd just filled and upending the contents all over the stall. "He thinks he's smarter than me. Him! That runt of an idiot. I know his game. He's been running errands for the duchessa, and he thinks he's God Almighty. But the duke's got wind of something and wants to know what his popish bastard wife is up to. So that's why I'm looking for the little weasel." At this point, he placed his foot in the middle of my chest and pushed down hard. I felt a crack and knew he'd broken a rib. He smiled. "I believe there are 23 more ribs I can break if you don't come clean with me now," and he prepared himself for another stomping.

"Stop," I screamed up at him. "I haven't got a clue. I've been watching him, too, to try and get my money back, but he's always coming up with some excuse. Believe me, Caporale, I'm with you on this," and I held the toe and heel of his boot, hoping beyond hope that he wouldn't stamp on me again.

He stood there poised above me, his black eyes darting this way and that as if trying to engage his brain in useful thought. Pulling his foot away, he turned and punched a hay bag, "I'm surrounded by fools and idiots."

"Look, boss," I said to him as I got to my feet, "if there are two of us looking for him, we'll catch him all the sooner. What do you think?" I added hopefully. If he took up my offer then I might at least be in a position to help Clare and Marco if they needed it. But my offer seemed to clutter his brain with too many suggestions, and he held his head as if it were going to explode.

"Life shouldn't be this complicated for a soldier," he moaned to himself. Then, as if he'd given birth to some great insight, he went on "OK. You come with me but if I find you've been double-crossing me, it'll be more than your ribs that I'll be cracking. Where did you last see the rat?" he spat at me.

I reached down to pick up my jacket and a small explosion went off in my chest. Standing up slowly and breathing shallowly, I told him all that I knew about Toni's domestic arrangements.

"Come on, then. We'll go and see if he's home. I've no doubt that we should be able to squeeze some information out of his friends and neighbors." By the sign of the evil snarl on his face, it certainly looked as if the caporale had regained his normal sadistic equilibrium.

Getting news of Toni's whereabouts proved to be more difficult than we both expected. Everyone seemed to know of him, but no one seemed to know where he was. I went to the taverna that I knew he frequented, sat at a table with the caporale, and waited. "You're getting as bad as he is with all this sitting on your backside and doing nothing," my irascible leader growled at me, whilst downing the contents of a mug of wine.

"Sometimes it's easier to let the news come to you instead of running around like a headless chicken trying to find something that you've no idea where it is," I growled back at him. "Toni may seem stupid, but he wasn't a complete idiot. He probably picked up more information by just sitting here watching and listening than most of the Duke's spies do by bribing people to give them information."

Pouring himself another mug of wine, the caporale looked at me sideways and muttered, "And maybe you ain't as stupid as you look either," and went to dig me in the ribs with his elbow.

"Don't," I shouted at him in anticipatory agony. "Please don't," I added when I saw the flare of anger in his eyes. "I think more clearly when my body isn't racked with pain" and attempted a weak smile. I could feel streams of sweat coursing down my chest and although I wanted to cough, the very thought of it sent cold shivers through every fiber of my body.

After some time, a man walked in who looked familiar to me. It had to be Toni's brother. I whispered this information in the caporale's ear. He started to get up, but I pulled him back and hissed, "Wait and watch." The man greeted the owner and asked if he'd seen his brother today. The owner's eyes immediately darted in our direction, but Toni's brother missed the signal.

"No, brother, he's not been in today," the owner said, whilst cleaning the wet mugs on the counter in front of him.

"If you do see him, just tell him that I'll be there." The owner looked confused.

"That's the message friend—'I'll be there.'" And turning on his heel, he left.

"Come on," I said, once he'd left the room. "Let's follow him and see where that leads us." The pain in my ribs had now turned into a blazing fire in my chest. Standing made my head feel dizzy and light, and even the caporale was worried enough to ask, "Are you alright?"

"Nothing that a week in bed with a good woman to feed me good food wouldn't fix," I answered, and beads of perspiration dripped from my forehead into my eyes. "Come on. We don't want to lose him now."

We headed out after him and followed him at a distance along the ever-emptying streets. He certainly wasn't going back to work, as the palazzo was in the other direction. He seemed to be heading out into the countryside. Then he disappeared.

"Where'd he go," I asked in amazement.

"Where all of us 'ave to go eventually," replied my friend, with a knowing nod. "Over there is the cemetery. Want me to see if there's a vacant spot for you, a'ter all, you do look a little peaky today." And the blow that he landed on my back felled me with a bolt of pain that racked my chest.

Gasping for breath as I slowly rose, I whispered, "That was not funny, Caporale, and we farmers have long memories."

"Stop your moaning, man," he hissed back, "otherwise I might just leave you here six feet under. Now look over there. Our friend seems to have business here. Someone seems to have taken your place in that hole in the ground. Looks like I'll have to put up with your whining for a little while longer."

Beyond the hedge that surrounded the small cemetery was a small cart next to a mound of freshly excavated earth. The jailer was standing next to it and staring into the abyss below him. A man's head popped up above the edge of the pit, and he threw a shovel onto the mound of clay. The jailer helped him out, and then the two of them lifted a bundle from the cart and unceremoniously dumped it into the grave. One of them spat into the hole, and the sound of laughter drifted across to the two silent watchers.

"Time to ask some questions, I think," the caporale said out of the corner of his mouth, then ducked through a gap in the hedge and set off toward the two men. The man with the shovel saw him first and set off like a frightened hare. The jailer had his back to us and this slowed his understanding of what was unfolding behind him. When he worked out what was happening, he turned to run, but tripped over the mound of clay and fell into the grave. The caporale, who had broken into a fast trot, slowed to a walking pace and burst out laughing at the same time.

Arriving at the edge of the grave, he peered down and said, "Two birds for the price of one, eh?"

"'Ow can I help you, Captain," asked the jailer, who was scrabbling to his feet.

"It's Caporale, not Captain, you idiot. Just tell me where Toni is," replied his tormentor, as he picked up the shovel and began to toss great clumps of earth over the poor man. The jailer tried to climb out over the side of the grave, but the caporale hit him a mighty blow on his hands, causing him to fall screaming back into the pit.

"Where's Toni, I asked?" he repeated, throwing another clod of clay into the face of the poor man.

"If you let me out, I'll tell you. Please, Caporale. Just let me out," he blubbered.

"This is the last time I'll ask you: where's that little rat of a brother of yours?"

"I dunno," screamed the poor man. "'E was supposed to be 'ere. Summink must've put the wind up 'im."

"And where do you think he might be going then," said the caporale, putting down the shovel and squatting by the side of the open grave.

By this time, the eyes of the jailer were almost popping out of his head with fear. "'E had a special consignment what 'e was takin' ta Rome. That's all I know. Honest. Please let me outta 'ere Caporale. It's not nice sittin' on top ov'a dead man in a dark grave. Please let me out." And he held up his hand for the caporale to pull him up. But the caporale didn't pull him up. He picked up the shovel, swung it high, and struck the man dead with a blow to his skull.

Turning to me, he said, "Come on. That is if you don't want to join your friend for a threesome." He grabbed the reins of the horse and cart and swung himself up into the driver's seat. Shouting over his shoulder, he said, "You sit at the back with the rest of the rubbish and keep your mouth shut, otherwise I'll fill it in for you." And flicking the whip, he told the horse to move on.

Sitting in the back of the cart was bone-wrenching agony to me. I felt each pebble that was crushed under those ironclad wheels, and before long, I fell into a swoon.

The cart had stopped. For how long I had no clue. Sweat filled my eyes when I opened them, making the shapes of trees swim and swirl. I went to sit up, and a thousand daggers dug deep into my chest causing me to grab the side of the ancient cart. My head rang, and my eyeballs throbbed with pain. As my head began to clear, I became aware of someone shouting nearby. I eased myself off the cart as gently as I could but almost fell to the ground as my legs buckled like a baby's. Holding on until I got my senses under control, I started off in the direction of the shouting.

Coming up behind a tall tree, I saw a terrible sight in the clearing in front of me. The caporale had a small girl around the waist and was holding his dagger at her throat. On the ground in front of him lay Toni, who had blood oozing into his hair from a nasty gash on his head. And standing a short way off was a stocky man with wild eyes who seemed paralyzed by fear for the girl, yet who looked powerful enough to rip the limbs off the caporale given half a chance.

I leaned against the trunk as the bells ringing in my ear became louder and louder. My clothes stuck to every part of me, seeing as they were drenched with the sweat pouring from my skin. I told myself that it was only five paces to where the caporale stood with his back to me, but another part of my mind screamed that it was a thousand miles of unbearable pain and I'd never make it. For a moment, everything around the edges of my sight became dark. The caporale seemed to turn and leer horribly at me. And the little girl whom he was holding changed and turned into my beautiful baby back home, who started to scream and scream and scream. Then the bells in my head stopped, it felt like a boulder had landed on my chest, and everything went black.

The dreams that followed were both terrifying and ecstatic. In the nightmares, the distorted face of the caporale would appear with blood leaking from his eyes, his teeth just inches from my face and holding the point of a dagger against my throat. At other times, I seemed to be floating on something soft. It felt like water, and yet I wasn't wet—and when I turned my head, I saw little people sitting on a wall looking at me and laughing. And yet, during this time of terrifying nightmares, sometimes I dreamt that a little angel would appear and wipe my head with an icy cloth that brought such sweet relief. Her little face would lean forward, and the light behind her made her seem almost transparent. Then she would kiss me ever so lightly on my forehead and disappear into the light.

I woke and thought I must be dead, so I began to pray for Maria and our baby. A light breeze stirred the lace curtain that framed the open window. It was so silent. Then I heard a chicken and began to chuckle at the foolish thought that there were chickens in heaven. It wasn't the best thing to do because the pain in my chest reminded me severely that I was definitely still alive and feeling decidedly mortal!

It may have been the gasp of pain that woke my angel, too, because her head appeared in the framed light of the window, and then disappeared immediately. I felt sad that she'd gone, because every time I'd seen her vision I had felt so much peace inside.

Then the door burst open, and my little angel appeared and came and knelt by my cot. "I am so happy to see you open your eyes," she said, and tears seemed to run down her cheeks.

"Am I still alive then?" I asked.

"Of course you are. And you saved all of us, too," she replied, wiping her tears away and smiling all the time. Then putting on a more serious face, "Now we don't want you to do any more damage to yourself. Marco will be in shortly to give you some soup, and maybe in a few days we'll carry you outside to get some sunshine, but in the meantime you stay here." And even though she only looked about 10 years old, the look in her eyes brooked no dissent!

"Just one question," I pleaded. "Where am I, and how did I get here, and is your name Clare?"

She smiled at me and said, "That's three questions! Rosso said you weren't very good at counting. Yes, I'm Clare, and you saved my life. And Marco's. And poor Toni's, too, but he's been almost as sick as you. He's on the mend now, too. Now enough talking and more resting," she ordered, shaking her finger in my direction like the little mother she was. Then she leaned down and the memory of my little angel's kisses flooded back as she kissed me on the forehead once more. And this time my own eyes filled with tears of happiness, washing away those bitter recent memories and nightmares.

One of the paradoxes of breaking your ribs—or in my case having your ribs broken for you—is that everything seems to be funnier! The drawback of laughing with broken ribs is that it HURTS. And believe me, that soon wiped the smile off my face. But all in all I surprised myself at how quickly I seemed to recover. It was a different situation for poor Toni, though.

The caporale had hit him on the head with the butt of his dagger, and the caporale was a mighty strong man. The blow had sent poor Toni reeling and had also removed a flap of skin from his head. Marco later told me that he thought Toni was dead. But the little man was tougher than we all expected. His wound healed, but he had a slight weakness in the left side of his body ever after.

"No more guard duty for me," he said to Marco with a weak smile one day.

"Well, I beg to differ," I interrupted him. "I've got lots of sheep back at my place that always need a sharp eye to guard them. That's if you're up to looking after fluffy things that don't want to kill you."

"I don't understand," Toni replied, looking genuinely perplexed.

"It's OK, Toni, I'll tell you more about it later. All I'm saying is that you don't have to worry about having a roof over your head because there's more than enough room at our place for a sharp-eyed ex-prison guard." And the smile that wreathed itself around young Toni's face was enough to make even an angel pause to smile.

We'd been staying at a small taverna on the edges of Imola, and as my strength returned, I asked Marco how we had all survived and what had happened to the caporale. Marco hung his head, and when he lifted it again, there was a look of shame on his face.

"I killed him," he said. "I had no choice, but I will feel guilty for the rest of my life that I took another man's life—but I had no choice!" He paused and ran his fingers through his hair as if trying to comb out the memory of it all. "He took us by surprise. He seemed to just appear whilst we'd stopped to take some refreshments. We'd been sitting there feeling so happy to be free and feeling the warmth of the sun on our faces—and then suddenly Toni's flat on his face with blood pouring from his head, and this leering giant has grabbed my beautiful Clare and is holding a dagger at her throat. The rage that filled me was matched by the paralysis I felt at seeing that blade at her throat. I've no idea what he was saying to me, because I was just waiting for him to make a mistake, and I knew I would kill him." Marco looked at me with his shame-filled eyes and said,

"That's a terrible thing to say, isn't it?"

"I don't think so, Marco, because one thing I do remember is thinking that he was holding my baby, and that's why I rushed at him," I answered.

Marco smiled and said, "Well, I can tell you that he certainly wasn't expecting that to happen! You unsettled him just enough for me to reach him before he did any damage, and then we fell to the ground wrestling over the knife. We rolled over a few times, and I suppose I must have turned the blade toward him on one of those turns because all I heard was the sound of air leaving his lungs and then all the life went out of him. It was so sudden and so unexpected. One second he was like a powerful animal, the next he was draped over me like a fallen tree."

"When I got up," he continued, "Clare was holding your head in her lap. We both thought the caporale must have stabbed you with his knife when you jumped on him. Then Clare realized that your body was burning with a fever, and that coughing was such an agony for you. Then we really got scared for you. I went to look at Toni, who was also in a terrible way, but he wasn't making any noise at all. He was still breathing, but he just lay there like a dead man. That's when my little Clare took charge. It was her idea to put you both into the cart and take you to the nearest town, where we could at least find a soft bed to put you in. Then she nursed the two of you for days on end. She's a very precious child, is our Clare." He said this whilst looking across at her as she sat and talked with Toni, who appeared to be having one of his better days.

"Toni told us that he knew you, but had no idea why you might be following us."

"Rosso," I replied, and he smiled back at me.

"If there's a mystery to be found, there always seems to be a redheaded monk in the middle of it," Marco quipped back. "Clare told me what had happened in the past. That was when Rosso and her went to Paris together. That's where he told her about you and the Dom and Ville-prieux. But we had no idea why you'd turned up out of the blue and saved all our lives."

I told Marco my story and the reason why I had left in search of the two of them. In retelling it all, I found myself amazed at how life can be so totally different from what you planned it to be. I never expected the twists and turns that had happened to me, and I certainly never thought I would be knocking on the doors of heaven, only to be pulled back by a young girl whose only gift seemed to be that of loving a stranger. And what a gift that had been for all of us.

We talked a lot, Marco and I, as I got my strength back, and the more I sat with him, the more I realized that he was an amazing man. He was so strong, and not just physically. The strength of the love that he shared with his Laura was enough to include the lost and the forgotten. A friendship was forged during those days that would last for the rest of our long days.

Then the time came for us to continue our journey back to Rome.

"I have a suggestion," I said, as we prepared to leave. "In a few days, when we start to cross the ranges, I propose that Toni and I head back to my farm. But on the way, there is something else I want to do. I want to pay a visit to someone. I can't tell you any more at the moment, but something tells me they are an important link to all of this."

Toni nodded in agreement and a rare smile warmed his face. "Sounds fine by me. I like sheep."

Rosso's
STORY

MOST OF THE greatest moments of our lives are totally out of our control from the moment we are born to the second that we die. We don't choose to be born, and we have no choice as to who our parents are. Likewise, death always comes too soon or too late, but rarely on time! The person we fall so deeply in love with is also unexpected and often totally different from the person you imagined them to be. The same is true when disasters happen, when friends are struck down in battle, or a little sister dies from an unlooked-for fever.

But opening that letter from Agnes was the biggest shock of my life. I had accepted little Anna's death because of the star that appeared in the sky. I couldn't comprehend how Agnes could write to me and tell me that she was leaving to marry another without ever having hinted at it in her previous letters. I was rocked with shock and overwhelmed with confusion. I read and reread that letter, and yet not one word of it changed or revealed what lay behind its contents. It was written in her hand and so I had to believe every word on the page. My heart was broken, and it was then that I truly understood how much I loved that woman. The only problem was that the realization had come too late.

I screwed the paper up into a ball and threw it into the corner. I walked around and around my cell, then stopped and picked up the crumpled ball and read it again. Nothing had changed, so I crumpled it again and tossed it aside for the last time. My eyes fell on the tome by my bed. It was the writings of William Flete. The monastery librarian had given it to me, and I had been intrigued by the contents. We live in this world of things and places, and yet so very often, those very things and places take control of our lives. William Flete was suggesting a radical change to how we monks should live our lives: give up our temples of plenty, walk away from endowments and the enmeshing power of rich benefactors, and embrace simplicity and poverty.

William Flete was an Augustinian just like me, and yet he perceived many things that had gone wrong with our Order. He wrote that "Worldliness is the ruin of the Order. The antidote is the practice of fraternal charity and fidelity to the common life in all its aspects, spiritual, intellectual and material." I wish I'd had the courage to tell our superior that! But William also realized that most of us monks lived in towns, cities, and villages "right in the middle of the market square, as well as in university centers." But then he said something that jumped off the page and into my head after I'd read Agnes's letter: "The friars should conduct themselves as if they were living in the desert."

The desert. Those two words rang in my ears. I needed to go into the desert. Looking back, I suppose a sort of madness descended on me then, and I joined some ideas together that at the time seemed blindingly obvious: William Flete, the desert, the world is in ruin.

I packed what few possessions I had left, and walked out of the monastery. A fleeting thought crossed my mind that I should let my friends know, but that was drowned by the idea that my burdens should not be their burdens, and that it would be unfair to disturb them with my plans. Perhaps, I deceived myself, I would write and tell them of my decisions later on, once I was settled.

Then I just started walking away from the city.

I had it in my mind that I would seek out William Flete, whom I believed was living in a forest near Siena. I would find him and live an eremitic life such as his. Then I would find peace. These were the holy thoughts that I tried to focus on whilst walking, but the image of my dear Agnes stood before me every step of that journey. And the perversity of it all was that she brought me great comfort and peace. Her decision to marry someone else confused me and gave birth to wild thoughts that danced in my mind like mad monkeys, but Agnes herself only begat the certainty of love in my heart.

In my journey towards Siena, it felt odd that I should be returning to where some of the most important events in my life had occurred. It was near Siena that I'd first met Villeprieux. It was not far from there that Gino had parted from us to live out his life with his long-lost love. It was near Siena where Dom had been tortured, and yet it was also near where my life was saved. But most precious of all, it was the place where I had met Agnes.

Now, here I was, so close to all those precious memories, and yet I was going to lose myself to the world by taking up the ways of a mystic. William Flete was going to be the key that would unlock a door in my soul and allow me to enter into a greater union with God. These were the lofty thoughts that I tried to fill my mind with on the road back to Siena.

Peace had returned to the area, and the countryside was at its glorious best as I walked along the dusty track that led to the city on the hill. The city's tall towers stood out against the brilliant blue skies, and birds swooped and sang as they hunted the insects that flourished in the heat. The forests were still thick at that time and often grew close to the path. They lent a cool canopy to those like me who travelled by foot. The occasional cart would rattle past, but mostly I was left to my isolation. When some kind soul did stop to offer a lift, I declined, having found great comfort in the cadence of my walking, which acted like an opiate to my senses. Fellow walkers ignored the dust-covered mendicant monk whose tonsured red hair was now matched by the redness in his mad eyes.

I was walking along a narrow, cobbled path lined by tall buildings before I realized that I had entered the city itself. The coolness of the shadows entered my consciousness at the same time as the echo of singing off those windowed walls. A group of men from one of the contrade was approaching, and I stepped to one side to let them past. Their singing was glorious, and they were very happy. They stopped at a small taverna close by and finished their song. As they called for wine, their merry laughter caused a smile to crease my dust-encased face.

"They're warming up for the Palio," a voice said in my ear. I turned to see who had spoken and found myself looking into the soft brown eyes of a washer woman who was carrying her load to be washed. I must have presented a weary and wild look, but she was a kind person who merely commented with a gentle grin, "You're new here, aren't you?"

"How could you tell?" I croaked back. These were the first words I'd spoken in days. "Is there somewhere I can find lodgings for the night?" I inquired. "I'm on my way to Lecceto," I added, as if that were information enough.

"Lecceto, is it?" she grumped. "I don't know what gets into you people's heads. You either go out to kill each other, or you run off and hide in caves, thinking you're going to have some ecstatic experience." And pulling her shawl over one shoulder and squeezing her laundry under the other, she turned and headed off down the street past the merrymakers. The last mutter I heard from her was "Men!" and then she coquettishly bowed her head whilst marching past her newfound admirers.

My legs had stiffened in those few minutes, and as I set off again, I felt like an old man. But soon I forgot my pains and immersed myself in the smells and the noise and bustle of Siena. Suddenly all the buildings vanished, and I found myself in a great piazza. Flags were draped from every building, and every face exuded a carnival expectancy. I'd heard about the Palio, and here I was in the very place where the horse race would be run. I turned to soak up every mote of the atmosphere, and I imagined what it would be like to be a rider on one of those horses, galloping around the piazza with thousands of people cheering me on.

Crowds of people were everywhere, and I was jostled along with them. To be touched by another human after such isolation thrilled me. The sweaty smells and the colors, the cacophony of the carnival, and the innocent delight in so many eyes were almost intoxicating. I no longer felt old. But I did feel hungry. It was a hunger that I hadn't experienced for some time. It was the hunger of a young man who wanted to fill his belly with food, not that of an austere monk who would offer up his fasting for a greater cause.

I sought out a place where I could sit and immerse myself in this experience and feed on fresh bread, cheese and a glass of wine. For that moment it was like a small piece of heaven. But a full stomach pricked my conscience, releasing the pent-up pain of my Agnes being married to another. It was as if a blood-caked bandage had been ripped from my heart. I pushed the last of the olives away from me and settled my account with the owner. I asked him whether he'd heard of Brother Flete. The look in his eyes confirmed that he thought he'd just fed a madman!

"Oh," he grunted, "you're another one of them, are you? What is it with you men? Can't you be happy here?" he said, waving his arms toward the milling crowd passing his taverna in the beautiful summer sunlight. Then tossing my few coins into his box, he accompanied me out into the street and gave me directions to the woods where I would find my English mystic. "And when you've tired of all that starving celibacy," he shouted after me as I departed, "come back and I'll give you a carafe of wine on the house, and the names of some beautiful women to entertain you." His words were met with lively laughter from his patrons and several passersby.

A shroud of loneliness descended on me again. Here I was in the middle of a beautiful city, surrounded by happy people, and yet I was heading out to find a cave and search for God. The idea that I might really be a little mad began to flit around inside my mind, but it was soon battered down by the steely decision that I must at least try to find what would truly give me happiness.

The walk out of Siena was a cleansing experience. Whilst in the town, I had felt the buzz of urban life with all its complexity. Yet as the houses and homes became fewer and fewer and the countryside blossomed around me, I felt like I was shedding a skin of envy and want. As the sun warmed me, and the sounds of the country replaced the blare of the city, I felt a peace envelop my thoughts. I felt reassured that I was making the right choice.

It's quite hard to find someone who prefers to live in silence and isolation. In fact, it took me some days of camping out under trees and begging from friendly farmers before I came close to the cliffs that rose above the woods surrounding them. As I approached the cliffs, the sounds of nature seemed to still themselves, and I became aware of the sounds of bees and the occasional fly on their hungry missions. I saw that there were several cave entrances in the cliff face. Nearby, at the edge of the woods, someone had built a tall monument of rocks with a small crucifix at the top. Around the monument was a well-trodden path edged with smooth white stones. Fresh petals had been scattered around the cairn, which gave the path a festive look. But of a human being, there was not a trace.

I caught myself in the act of calling out for anyone who might be there, but I stopped midbreath out of respect for the sonorous silence of the place. I began to slowly follow the path around the special edifice until I became mesmerized by the face of that terrible crucifix, which stared down at me in all its agonized glory.

Perhaps it was the magic of the place or perhaps the simple fact that I was totally exhausted after my travels and the scant food I had eaten along the way: whatever the reason, I fell into a deep sleep that was devoid of any dream whatsoever.

I woke with a start in the middle of the night and all around was deep darkness. Above, the night sky reassured me with its twinkling humor. I looked towards the cliff and saw the low glow of a golden light coming out of one of the caves, and I knew that Brother Flete was there. I made to stand up, but thought better of it. The Hermit was a holy man, and I must wait on him, not the other way around, I thought. I went to lie back down, but then I smelt fresh bread: a small loaf had been left near where I slept. The hermit knew I was here, and he would come to me in his own good time.

The night was still, and all I could hear was the silence ringing in my own ears. Then an owl hooted from its haunt, its sound so pure that in my muddled mind, I thought it must be a sign from God. The owl hooted several times more, and each time I waited hopefully for just one more hoot. Then the owl ceased calling, and I felt the inner shadow of loneliness envelop me once more. I lay on my back and tried to imagine where the owl had gone and what it looked like. I wondered whether it had seen me. But I was answered by silence, whilst the stars stared down from the black heavens above.

I woke early in the morning with a film of dew on my clothes. It must have been the sound of singing that woke me. Not the silvery sound of the dawn chorus, but of a man singing his morning office. I got up and worked my stiff limbs until they moved freely, then headed off in the direction of the song. It came from the same cave that I'd seen illuminated on the previous night, so I went and waited near the entrance.

"Do come in and join me, Brother," a voice called out in accented Italian. I pulled my cowl around my shoulders and went inside. The contrast between the bright light of dawn and the dullness of the cave caused me to stop and adjust to the much-reduced light level. As if coming out of the darkness, an image slowly appeared, took on human form and became a man. I was surprised to see him in a singlet and trousers. His beard was long, thin, and unkempt. He had long slender fingers such as musicians have who play the lute, but it was his eyes that garnered my attention. They were blue like the starling's egg, but flecked with sea green. They held my attention as if they sought something hidden inside me.

"This is the most wonderful time of day, Brother, and it just demands that we sing a song of praise. Come. Join me," and he indicated a small pile of dry ferns near the mouth of the cave where the two of us sat and sang our morning office. Outside, the wild world responded with songs of its own.

When we had finished, we shared the small loaf that I had found during the night, but no words were spoken while we ate.

"I've come looking for something Brother William, but I'm not sure if I've come to the right place."

He chuckled for a moment and said, "None of us knows where to look, Brother, and most of us fail to see the answer even when it's in front of us. But the great thing is to dare to ask the question in the first place. Somewhere in the Bible, our Lord tells his disciples to 'push your boat out into the deep.' It's a message for all of us for all times. Dare to take a risk, move out of our comfort zones, and question our teachings and our beliefs. Some things that may have worked for others in the past don't work anymore, so we must lay them aside and adapt and change. Just because we dare to try something different doesn't make it wrong. Each age calls for renewal, and our age is no different from all those that have gone before. Our Master was the best example of that. He took on the hierarchy and offered a new way forward. But he knew it would be hard, and he knew the consequences of his actions. He was crucified. Don't be drawn in by the comfort of faith, most of us will suffer to some degree or other for following in his footsteps."

Brother William paused and turned those pale blue eyes on me and apologized. "I'm sorry," he said, "It's been some time since I've had anyone to talk to." He allowed a smile to dissolve his concern and added, "And when I do have someone to talk to, then the words just seem to pour out of me."

My silence seemed to reassure him. "If you're going to stay on, I can highly recommend the cave next door. Well, it's not actually next door, more a hundred yards further along. It's a rather nice little cave, actually," he chatted in his English accent. "The last occupant managed to stay for almost a month before he discerned that perhaps our Lord had other ideas for him. You're welcome to it, if you want it."

"Thank you, Brother," was all I could manage, then we returned to sitting in silence at the mouth of the cave, just watching the world change its hues and scents and sounds. Measuring time seemed pointless in William's presence, so I don't know when it was that I slowly rose and made to leave.

"Take the rest of the bread with you," William said, "I have a second small loaf that I always keep in reserve, just in case I have visitors." The merriment in his eyes made me burst out laughing. "You need it more than me at the moment. There is fresh water in the stream down below. But be warned, most people seem to get a spot of dysentery when they first drink it. I did when I first arrived, but it doesn't worry me now. I seem to remember that one poor fellow almost died from it. There are also plenty of herbs, nuts, mushrooms, and berries to be had if you're prepared to search for them." For the son of a butcher, this sort of diet was not an appealing prospect.

"The good news is that the priory does send someone around every few days with some supplies. Apparently the abbot thinks it's not good for the community if his monks starve to death in the woods. Mind you," he said, with that merry twinkle returning to his eyes, "Mother Church does love her saints and martyrs, doesn't she?" With that, he placed the remains of the small loaf in my hands and pointed me in the direction of my new home.

As a child, I grew up walking in the woods, and so I knew many of the trees, plants, and animals that lived there. The woods also held unpleasant memories of my father, but for the moment such memories were a long way from my mind. Even so, there's a huge difference between walking through a wood and actually thinking of living in it. For the moment, though, I was filled with zeal and eager to experience the ecstatic life that I'd read about in the monastery in far-off Rome.

I found my cave and went inside. It was small and dry, although the temperature was several degrees colder inside than it was outside. There were obvious signs of old fires near the mouth of the cave, and a small pile of dry kindling at the rear of my new home. A patch of dried ferns indicated where the previous occupant had lived, so my first job was to kick that into a pile. I planned to burn it later, just in case it harbored any unwelcome inhabitants. Then I went outside again to explore.

The woods near Siena cover much of the countryside, but they are what I would call working woods. I found snares laid to catch rabbits and small birds. There were also trails created not by human feet, but by the bustling bulk of wild boar. These beasts can explode out of the scrub and have been known to gore a man to death, so I was wary of their possible presence. I needed dry bedding, and ferns were best for that, so I gathered what I thought to be enough for a man of my size. I would also need water and something to carry it in. It took me half a day to find a piece of hollowed-out wood that I could use to transport water to store in my cave overnight. During my searches, I picked various berries and nuts that I knew were safe to eat and put them in my pocket.

I returned to my cave and set my meager comestibles in a safe place. I put a spark to the old fern bed and went outside to sit and pray whilst the smoke and any small beasties disturbed by the fire could disappear outside. Clouds threatening rain were gathering near the horizon. At least I had a dry cave and some food, so I was content to settle and soak up the isolation.

To the novice, the attraction of living like a hermit appears quite wonderful: No more distractions, no more noise, just you and the Almighty—alone together. But that's where the first real challenge arises. For the imminent challenge is not the awesome presence of the Almighty and the supposedly thunderous judgment He is about to make on your life up until the present moment.

No, the almost impossible challenge is to quiet your own mind long enough to allow the Master of the Universe to actually come into your presence! The struggle to achieve inner silence begins as soon as you stop doing things. Our minds, it seems to me, were meant for action. My attempts to change the habits of a lifetime and simply be still opened the door to deep, dark thoughts that I never knew existed inside me. And my dreams during that time were terrifying to the point that I was almost fearful of going to sleep.

In one nightmare, I opened the door into Agnes's cottage. She stood there looking as beautiful as ever. I could feel the warmth of her hands on my face, I could smell and hear the sounds of her clothes. I could see the small scars on her beloved face, and I could bathe in the loving light from her eyes. In the next moment, a man was standing close and talking animatedly to her and clasping his hands behind her neck. She seemed both frightened and exhilarated. The man had his back to me, and then he turned to face me. It was Villeprieux, and he smiled that friendly smile of his. For some reason, I could see his fingers, and they were long with filthy nails and smeared with blood. I could feel myself beginning to burn with anger. I saw him dig those fingers into Agnes' neck. She smiled up at Villeprieux. He continued to look at me, and then I saw that his eyes were shot red with blood. I instantly hated him deep in my soul and screamed "Leave her alone." And as I screamed, I sat bolt upright and woke up gasping for air with sweat pouring down my back.

Some days after this dream, which had really rattled me, I went to William's cave to talk with him. "I heard you screaming the other night," he said. In the silence that followed, I half expected that he would say something to calm my mind. But he didn't.

"It's not easy being a Christian, you know. Wouldn't it be wonderful if there was a simple formula that led to perfection or to heaven on Earth? But sadly, there aren't any shortcuts. What I do here may work for me, but I suspect that it wouldn't work for many others. Each generation needs to find where God is working in their lives. What worked in the past may not work now. Catherine can see it. Francis has seen it, too. What our Master spoke of in Galilee is almost unrecognizable these days. Over the centuries it's become encrusted with rules, traditions, power and wealth. We need to clear away the old wood and continue the ongoing work of renewal that each of us is called to do." Whilst he was speaking, there was no harshness in his voice, just a sense of calm.

"You will probably find that your dreams will become more vivid when you fast and suffer. I see it as peeling away the layers that we cover our soul with. But not all dreams do that. Sometimes they are things of complete beauty and remind us of what it is to be loved and to love others. I am not a dream interpreter. I am a simple man following a simple way. If I am an example for others, then so be it. If I am a source of annoyance to others, then so be it. I prefer simplicity to complexity. I prefer service to power, and I love this wood and this cave. I will be sad to leave when the time comes for me to go." He looked out over the trees, and the wind gently and benevolently sighed into his face.

If the dream disturbed me, then the dysentery nearly killed me. I'd been drinking water that had collected in a small hollow in a rock near my cave, but when that had dried up, I drank from the stream. The cramps came first, and then the diarrhea. I had no idea you could lose so much foul fluid so quickly. My tongue cleaved to the roof of my mouth, and I was driven half-mad with thirst. I became delirious, but remained lucidly aware of the times when William came and tended to me. He reminded me so much of my gentle Agnes. The paradox of those few days of delirium were that I had a dream that has sustained my life ever since.

The dream started, as they all do, without any introduction. I found myself in a vast white cloud, such as you see in thunderclouds before they become dark and threatening. I was in the middle of an enormous mass of whiteness with thrilling eddies of softness that swept me higher and deeper into its very substance. I knew instinctively that the cloud was made of pure love. And I knew that I could not live and experience so much love. My lungs felt as if they were going to explode. Then I woke up.

Reflecting on the dream, I came to believe that God's love is like that— infinite. In this life, we cannot comprehend how much God loves us. For me, that dream has become like the sound of the owl in the wood. We only need to hear it once to know it exists, yet we keep going back to the same spot in the hope of hearing it again. Brother William, in his own simple way, was trying to teach us that we don't have to keep going back to the same spot to find God or hear the owl. He's everywhere. But we do need to learn to pause so that we can clear our minds of our accumulated dead ideas and make time for Him to come to us.

I recovered from the dysentery, but it left me very weak, and I remained close to my cave for some time afterwards.

William came to me one day and said, "I'm leaving soon. Catherine has died," and he smiled a beautiful smile. "Imagine no more suffering. Imagine being in a place that is so full of love that . . . ," and his search for words failed him.

"So full of love that you cannot breathe?" I finished for him.

He looked me in the eye for what seemed like an age, but was perhaps only a few seconds, then softly replied, "You heard the owl."

We clasped each other in complete joy, then he went on, "I am going back to England. My time here is over, but my mission is only just beginning. There is still so much work to be done. One day we will meet merrily again, but not on this earth. I wanted to thank you, Rosso, for your earnestness. Stay as long as you need to." As he said that, he had an unfathomable expression on his face. "But now you know what love is and where to find it, too." Reaching out, he tapped my chest lightly over my heart.

We embraced once more like dear brothers, and then he left. My last sight of him was him going down the slope, away from my cave, and into his beloved woods. He was and is a great man, and I will always love him.

Life seemed to be calling me away, moving me on, and now I had a clearer picture of my future. I did stay on for several days afterwards. I had made up my mind about my future but wanted to linger in that place for the very simple reason that I could!

On my last day, I visited all the spots that I had grown to love and paused before the small stone altar with the crucifix on top. I turned towards where I had first seen the golden glow from William's cave, and my footsteps took me in that direction one last time. This small paradise seemed so empty without his presence. He'd left the cave clean and tidy, even to the point of replacing his fern bed and stacking dry kindling at the back, well away from the entrance. Then I noticed a small pile of neatly folded clothes with a small note on top, held down by a marble stone. In the pile were his tunic and trousers. I smiled at the thought of him going to cold England without any clothes, but he would have had his Augustinian habit safely stowed since his arrival. In my mind, I saw his slight frame in that black habit and prayed that the smell of the wood would stay with him forever.

I picked up the note and found it was addressed to me. Opening it, I read in Latin, "*Habeo Sententia haec tibi necessaria—Willelmus*" (I have a feeling you will need these—William.)

He knew, even before I had made the decision, that I would not be taking my final vows.

My faith had been deepened and enriched by so many experiences in life, but I was called to live out my life in the world, not in a monastery. With that decision came great relief, even though it opened up so many unknowns.

In the last few days, I had decided that I would travel back to Rome. I would call past where my dearest Agnes used to live, because during my blessed time in the wood I had come to realize that I had heard the owl twice in my life. However, when I first heard it, I was too naive to understand what it was. I now knew that I loved Agnes more than anything on this earth, and I would do all I could, wherever I could, to make her happy, even if I had to do it in secret. As she was married now, being close to her would be impossible, but there would be other ways I could make her and her family's life easier. I would become her silent benefactor and pray for her every day for the rest of my life.

I took off my old habit and put on William's tunic and shirt. I went to the stream and washed my scent out of the black cloth and left it in the sun to dry, just as a snake leaves its old skin behind in spring. Later I folded it neatly and went back to William's cave to spend my last day there. I thought I might have some special dreams that last night, but I slept like a baby, and any dreams evaporated with the blaze of the rising sun.

My journey took me back through Siena, where I stopped at the taverna. The owner gave me a double take before coming over with a cup of wine and some olives. "On the house," he said with a smile. "It'll make your hair grow," he smiled as he brushed his hand over my tonsure. "Seen the light, have you?"

"Seen it?" I replied. "I've been in it."

"So you found your William then, eh?"

"Found him. Lost him. But found my future, and it looks pretty good from where I'm sitting now."

"Welcome back to the real world," my host chuckled. "It may not be perfect, but it sure beats the alternative." Flipping his towel over his shoulder, he turned and approached a young lady who had just arrived. "And what may I do for you, Princess?" he asked, with an almost lecherous sound to his voice.

Later that same afternoon I was walking close to where Agnes used to live. I had determined that I would pause at the end of her road, as there was no point in going to the cottage because it would be cold and empty, haunted by old memories and mice. I preferred my memories to be warm and my own. So I was mildly surprised to see smoke coming from her chimney. "Strange," I thought to myself and began to walk slowly towards the building.

All seemed as if I'd just come back from hunting for fresh meat when I'd stayed with her. The garden beds were well cared for, and there were even chickens in the newly erected coop close by the house. A cow rattled its bell in the small green field by my path and raised its moon eyes to stare at me. It held my gaze and appeared to be saying, "Ah, you're back," as if it had long expected me. Then it went back to ripping the green grass from its roots.

I went and stood by the door, not knowing what lay behind. I knocked and waited.

She opened the door. Her eyes opened wide, her hands flew to her mouth to suppress a scream, then she burst out crying and laid her sobbing head on my shoulder.

My concern for her overcame all the confusion that swirled in my mind. My Agnes was sobbing on my shoulder, and that one fact occupied all the time and all the space in the universe for me. I held her. I smelt the sweet smell of her hair next to my face. I felt the heaving of her shoulders slow as her hand reached down to her pocket for a handkerchief. Then there were just the two of us, warm against each other--the two most complete hearts in all the world.

Agnes raised her head, and her face was just inches away from mine. Her eyes glistened with fresh tears, but it was the smile on her face that melted all my wounds, all my cares away. Then wiping her eyes, she said in her quiet, familiar way, "Forgive me, Rosso, for being so emotional. But it's been such a long time, and it was so very unexpected. But don't stand here on the doorstep, come inside, you must be famished from your travels."

"But your husband," I stammered.

"My husband?" she replied in honest confusion. "I'm not married, dearest of brothers. Whatever gave you that idea?" I was thrown into deeper confusion by her response and jarred by her calling me "brother."

"Oh, Agnes," I said, reaching out and holding her by the arms. "Forgive me for the blindness of my youth. How could I ever think of you as my sister when I love you so dearly with the whole of my heart, every fiber of my body: you who are the completion of my soul and the very reason for my existence. Forgive me, dearest Agnes. Forgive me." Now it was my turn to bury my head in her shoulder and sob all my foolishness away onto that gentle place of comfort.

When I had finished, she smiled and offered me her handkerchief, saying, "I think you need it more than me now." Our eyes both sparkled as we laughed and embraced again. "With all this crying, I think we'll need to drink as much as we eat," Agnes said gently, pushing me away and heading toward her cupboards. "But tell me, whatever gave you the impression that I was married?" she asked, as she poured water from a stone jar into two mugs.

"Your letter," I answered in compete innocence. "The letter you wrote to say that you had met someone else and that you were going off to marry him."

Agnes paused what she was doing, a puzzled expression caused her brow to wrinkle and then, in a moment, a truth was revealed to her.

"I never wrote that letter, Rosso." It was my turn to look stunned.

She turned her pure and honest face towards me and said, "My dearest Rosso. Since the moment I found you, I swore to myself that I would never be with any other man until I drew my last breath. I have loved you every second of every hour since that moment."

The great fullness in my throat rose up and erupted into tears which washed away any lingering doubts. "Oh, my dearest and most blessed love. How big a fool have I been?" In two swift paces, she was back in my arms, and we were both convulsed by love, laughter, and tears.

Drying her eyes once more, she said happily, "Enough of this nonsense. Sit down and let me get some food for you, and we'll talk once your stomach is content."

"We might be in for a long period of silence then," I replied cheekily.

"Shh, you," she rounded on me. "Some things never change, and one of them is your cheek, Master Rosso. Or is it Brother Rosso now?" She looked at my tunic and added, "But I'm not sure which order you belong to."

"The Holy Order of Agnes," I replied, looking up from the plate of food she had placed in front of me. "And I'm afraid I've entered for life."

No artist in all the land could have captured the look on my Agnes's face. I now knew the balance of scarred yet sacred beauty with pure love and happiness was mine alone. I was honored in that moment.

We sat and ate at her table in her small neat kitchen in her humble house, and we were the happiest people in the whole world. I have no recollection of what I ate. What I do remember is that I would take a bite, chew my food, and look at her. Smiling and masticating are not comfortable bedfellows, but I recall plenty of smiling. For her place, Agnes seemed content just to sit and look at me and smile and giggle. At one point, she reached forward and wiped a crumb that had escaped my attention and was hiding at the corner of my mouth. It was such a simple action. But whilst so many events of my life have been lost to my mind, if I ever feel low, all I need to do is recall that moment, and love and happiness flow back into me.

With the meal over, we took ourselves outside and slumped down against the wall in the late evening sun—just like in old times.

"I've been thinking about what you said. About that terrible letter. I think I know how that came about," Agnes said. She half-turned toward me and reached out to hold my hand in both of hers. "A young man came by who suffered from the falling sickness. I think I wrote to you about him," she said and saw the confirmation in my eyes. "I took him in because he had nowhere else to go. He told me he'd been a copyist and scribe for a lawyer who'd treated him unfairly. He seemed such a simple and honest person." She paused and in that short silence she struggled to find words to capture his deceit. "Let me just say that he wasn't as honest as he appeared at first glance. For a time, all went well, and he helped a little around the place. He made fine copies of the books that Father Alphonsus had sent me. It was impossible to tell the difference between the original and the facsimiles. But he was a hopeless hunter, unlike the present company," and her hands squeezed mine a little harder. I shrugged my shoulders and looked suitably smug at her compliment about my trapping skills.

"Soon he started to act as if it were his house, and I was his guest. He never harmed me physically, but he took advantage of my compassion, which is sometimes a more hurtful wound than an actual blow." It was my turn to squeeze her hand. She responded with a loving smile and went on. "One day I came back from visiting a neighbor. There was no one home, so I came back immediately. He was there in my room, looking at my letters. I felt betrayed and went in and confronted him. First, he tried to bluff his way out with contrived stories, and I was wavering on the point of believing him when he mentioned that Father Alphonsus was dead." There was a look of confusion on her face and hurt, too. "I had not received any letter from the dear man in months and couldn't work out how the young man knew such a thing. But one lie led to another, and soon even he was lost in a maze of deceit of his own making."

We are all called to forgive the sins of those who trespass against us, but few of us have the capacity to really do that. Agnes could. She had forgiven that troubled man who'd deceived her and used her badly.

The sun had slipped behind the horizon, and the lingering evening light seemed reluctant to draw back from our presence. "I don't know why he felt that lying was necessary. I would have helped him anyway," she said, in that wise way of hers. "He was only a boy in a man's broken body, and I suppose he protected the little boy in him by lying. He would have seen plenty of examples of how it had been successful for others who had accumulated great wealth and power," she said. A shiver caused her to tremble. "Perhaps we'd better go in. I think there will be a heavy dew tonight." I stood and pulled her to her feet and held her in my arms whilst studying her face. Yes, there was real love for me there, but there was also the receding shadow of a recent hurt. Perhaps she'd shivered because it was getting cold, or perhaps it was at the memory of a young man who'd lost his moral compass.

We went back into her home, lit some candles, and sat opposite each other at the kitchen table--holding hands! "Something caused him to change recently," she went on. "He'd become nervous and more fretful. He'd raise his voice to me, which is something he'd never done before. But he never harmed me," she added quickly as she saw anger flicker in my eyes. "It was after a stranger arrived at the door one day. He never told me who it was or what it was all about. Just that some vagrant came, which had made him feel that we were unsafe out here all on our own."

Agnes has a heart big enough to love the whole world. I had been blessed enough to be the one destined to love, and be loved, by her. Yet people who love like Agnes not only have great hearts, they have unquenchable spirits. They can look into the eyes of even the most dangerous of people and dare to challenge them with the truth.

"He knew before I told him that he couldn't stay with me any longer. He had stopped looking me in the eye when I spoke with him. I tried to find a spark of honesty in him, but his lies became more devious and eventually all effective conversation finished between us. I told him to leave, and the words actually hurt him. Maybe it was the little boy in him that had dared to come forward for a second, but if so, the boy was soon beaten back by the more malicious man he'd become. He told me 'you'll pay for this,' whatever that threat may mean, although I think I know now. He wrote it. And then he just disappeared one day without a trace."

The guttering candle set shadows dancing around the room. Her eyes looked sad as if she'd failed in some way.

"When I was lost, my dearest Agnes," I began, "I met two men who began to change my life. But they didn't complete the job. You completed my life, and I thank God every day for that now. You did as much as you could for that sad man, but it's now up to other good people to bring him to the point of change and completion. It might take a hundred such encounters before healing comes to him, or he may harden his heart to the whole world and refuse to change. But you, my beloved, have done all that you could, and you should be at peace with that."

I had been staying with Agnes for some time, and my hair had begun to cover the top of my head.

Agnes had even managed to trim it into an acceptable appearance. Suddenly there was a loud banging at the door. Agnes's face went white, her worried eyes looked at mine, and she whispered, "Do you think he's come back?"

"Shh," I hissed softly and indicated that she should go into her room and close the door. I was walking to the door when the loud knocking came again. I moved the covering on the window next to the door, but could only see the back of a stocky man. Taking a deep breath and bracing myself, I swung the door open.

Afterwards, we both laughed until tears streamed down our faces, because neither of us could believe what we were seeing. "I thought your mouth would never shut again this side of Paradise," Gino said, struggling to regain enough breath to speak.

"I thought you'd taken root and would start sprouting leaves, you looked so thunderstruck," I replied, finding it hard to stop the laughter-induced pain in my belly and breathe at the same time.

By this time, Agnes had appeared, and her eyes were illuminated with joyous wonder. "Agnes, my love, this is the most wonderful friend a man ever had. This is Gino. I thought I'd never see him again, and here he is knocking at your door. Will wonders never cease?" And the three of us embraced as only the closest of friends can. "But what am I saying? Come in, come in," I said to Gino, and the three of us went and sat around the simple wooden table that had seen and heard so many tales.

We talked long into the night, and many a candle was sacrificed to that happy reunion. Agnes, sensing that dawn would soon be upon us, made up two beds for us by the fire before she retired to her own room. Gino and I carried on talking until the sparrow's song suggested we get some sleep—which meant it was late in the day when we eventually woke again.

Of Agnes there was no sign, which caused a flurry of anxiety to pass through my mind. But she appeared about the time that Gino's stomach and mine had decided it was time to be fed, and the good woman produced fresh bread that she had purchased from the farmer nearby.

"I also asked him if his son could look after the place for a few weeks," she said archly, "because I suspect that there may be one more journey for the two of you to make."

Gino and I looked at each other. "I told you she was a mind reader." I laughed. "Tell us, my dear, where do you think we might be going, then?"

Agnes looked at us both with mock wounded pride before going on, "Well, if I were a couple of friends who'd heard that their friends had been in all sorts of trouble, then I would like to know that they had gotten home safely. And if they weren't home safely, then I'd want to go and help them." Sitting, she glanced from one to the other to confirm that she had hit her mark.

"Whatever you do, Rosso, make sure that you marry this woman," Gino whispered in my ear.

"What are you two plotting now?" Agnes smiled back at us.

"Nothing," we replied in perfect unison, and we all laughed loud and long.

The journey to Gino's place took a few days, but we weren't rushing, rather we were rejoicing in each other's company. I also had the pleasure of Agnes being constantly at my side.

Maria was the first to spy us. She had long been watching for Gino's return. Toni was happily ensconced in the little shepherd's hut up on the hillside. "He's a different person from the man who arrived here a few weeks ago," Maria said, glowing with happiness. "And it's not just getting his strength back. Something's come alive in him. He'll be so glad to see you, Gino."

"And I'll be glad to see him, too. But not a tenth as glad as I will be to see my beautiful Bella. Where is she?" I said.

"You're not going to believe me," said Maria, with one eyebrow cocked higher than the other. "Rabbit's changing her diaper!"

"What?" Gino shouted in amazement. "What is the world coming to?" he cried in wonderment. Agnes and I looked at each other in confusion.

"They say it takes a little while, but babies eventually manage to train their parents!" Maria said, grinning at Agnes. "Rabbit's the name of the lost soul who brought us the message from Dom," she said as an aside. "He's a good lad despite his appearance."

"Changing diapers, though, Maria. It's not a good thing for the male reputation. Just wait until I've had a word with the young fellow." Gino smiled at his beloved.

"Oh, stuff and nonsense," she said, pushing playfully away from an approaching hug. "Come inside, all of you, and let's get you fed properly." And following the dear lady into the house, we all submitted to her motherly attentions. Toni arrived shortly, having seen our group arrive from the distant hillside. His reunion with Gino was very emotional. After they had embraced, they stood at arm's length smiling like two awkward teenagers, and they embraced once more. Gino introduced Toni to Agnes and me. It was a delight to meet someone who had been a part of rescuing our dear friends, and we thanked him from the bottom of our heart. "I've found a new life, unlike my brother of blessed memory. Now I have new friends, a new family, and I'm happy," he said. "What more could a man want?"

What more indeed, I thought to myself.

But our destination wasn't Gino's farm and family, it was Rome, and it was dear Maria who reminded us of that after she'd filled our stomachs to the point of bursting. "What time will you leave tomorrow, husband?" she asked from the trough where she rinsed the platters.

"I couldn't leave you so soon," the poor man blustered in some discomfort, much to the delight of the rest of us watching.

"Gino, my love, you can't leave a job half completed," she said, coming over to him and putting her arms around his waist. "I know you're torn, but the sooner you start, the sooner you'll get home again." She reached up and kissed him gently on the lips, then placed her finger there as if to seal the memory of it in his mind.

"You're right," replied Gino, "and at least you've got two fine men to protect you until I get back." This time it was his turn to return her embrace and love.

We headed south about midmorning, intent on reaching Rome in a few days if we were lucky and the weather held. There was an anxiety about the trip, yet it was mingled with the great delight that Gino and I were on the road again, reliving old memories, and we were in the company of the dearest woman in the whole world: my Agnes.

Eventually we trudged down the slopes from Hadrian's ruined old palazzo and made off across the plains to Rome itself. There we joined the throngs entering the gates and made straight for Gian's taverna, where all news eventually settles after the storms of life. He was delighted to greet us and immediately sent for Brother Julian at Santa Maria Maggiore "on urgent family business." The three of us were immediately submerged in a flow of family and food. Gian's wife took Agnes under her wing and straight out to the kitchen where they could "discuss things" in peace and quiet.

"I've heard that Laura and the children are back, as well as their friend. But there's still no news of Marco and Clare," Gian reported, after finishing a plate of excellent pasta.

"And the Dom?" I asked. Gian's brow furrowed. Before he could answer, the sound of joyful singing came from the alleyway, burst through the front door, and then filled our room and hearts with great happiness. Julian had arrived.

The glorious welcome that was such a natural part of that home was repeated once more, and all the children were treated as equals when it came to love and attention.

"Welcome home," Julian fired, whilst perching his ever-increasing girth on his favorite chair. "What a great blessing you bring to this house." He paused as Agnes stood before him and gazed into her eyes. Without turning away, he said to me, "There is no doubt in my mind, Rosso, where your true vocation lies." Then he enveloped her in his arms and kissed her tenderly on both cheeks. "Welcome, dear lady."

"Thank you, Brother Julian. I feel that I've known you all of my life. You've been such a blessing to all of us." He smiled happily back into her almost-perfect features. Then he sniffed, turned, and cried, "Food," and his eyes opened with mock wonder. "Dear brother, we'll keep you poor if you feed us like this all the time."

"As we didn't have a fatted calf, dear brother, I thought a modest feast might do instead," replied Gian merrily.

We all sat around the table, and Gian's wife joined us, "seeing as it's such a special occasion." She seated herself next to Agnes so they could continue their whispered conversation. None of us had noticed that Gian's eldest son was not amongst us, but after the first bowl of food had steadied our hunger, there was knocking at the door. "Who could that be?" said Gian, looking worried. "I'll be back in a moment," he said, and he rose and left the room. The conversations continued in a subdued, listening fashion. A noise of scurrying feet sounded and then what sounded like mice squeaking.

The door opened to reveal two boys in black capes, followed by the regal presence of Sarah, who was followed by Laura, friend Connie, and bringing up the rear, the two smiling faces of the conspirators, Gian and his eldest son. "I knew we couldn't have a feast without Laura and her family," he said, whilst helping his son drag another table next to the main one. Once again there was great joy in the room and dear friends embraced, laughed, and even shed the odd tear.

There was a gleam of light in Laura's eyes which nothing could hide. "What is it?" I asked.

There was more noise in the corridor. Then there before my eyes stood Marco, holding Clare's hand and looking fit to burst with happiness.

"They just got back this morning," said Laura, immediately going to her husband's side and reaching for his hand. I walked slowly around the throng until I stood in front of Clare. She seemed to have blossomed into a young lady, yet she still had the wise eyes I'd seen over what seemed like an eon ago. "Welcome home" was all I could muster before we both embraced and wept into each other's hair.

Sniffling and turning at the same time, I introduced Clare to Agnes. There was only a head of height difference between the two of them, and for a moment, I thought they might be sisters. "It's so good to meet you at last," said Clare politely, "Rosso's told me all about you. In fact he's told us all about you." Everyone laughed, Agnes blushed, and I held her in my arms.

"Don't think you can have all the fun without me," a familiar voice shouted from without.

"Uncle Dom!" The children screamed and ran to meet him. Gian smiled quietly.

"Have you been plotting again, brother?" said Julian.

"Maybe a minor intrigue," replied his twin, "but nothing worth reporting to the great Boss on high," he smiled. "Dom came back a few days ago. He and his companions met up with Rosso's William Flete on their journey south. He told them about Rosso. Then Dom's Cathar friends decided to accompany Brother Flete back across the Alps, and so Dom came on home to Rome. Since then we've been trying to hide him, which is no mean feat! He's been staying in peaceful isolation with Pietro, but I think he's missed the children."

Pietro came in first, leaning on his cane, without needing his beads. That made us all happy. Then came Dom, draped in writhing humanity and surrounded by the sounds of happy giggling. He looked down at us all with a huge smile on his face. Then his expression changed as if he'd been struck on the head, and a look of great shock filled his face. He stared across the room, and we all turned to see what he was looking at.

What we saw was Agnes with a similar look on her face. She was the first to recover, saying almost under her breath, "Bruno? Could it really be you, Bruno?" as she walked slowly toward him. For his part, Dom had disentangled himself from the small ones and was saying "Ann? What are you doing here?"

"You know each other?" I asked incredulously.

"He's my brother," said Agnes as she fell into his arms, and they sobbed with great delight.

In all the confusion and emotion, it took some time to fit all the pieces together. Laura comforted Agnes as she told her story, and Gino and I stood with Dom as he filled in his part. It was stunningly simple, really. Agnes had told me from the beginning that her name was Ann Agnes, but she preferred the name Agnes. For his part, Dom, or Bruno, had taken the name of his beloved Poppa just in case anyone had cared to follow him in those far-off days when he and Agnes first fled from their home. After that, he'd just stuck with the name.

My joy couldn't have been greater. Here I was with my beloved Agnes, my friends had all returned safely, and now Dom was to become my true brother—for I had determined that I would marry Agnes, and marry her soon.

"A toast," Gino shouted above the din, "To Rosso and Agnes! To love and family!"

And we all shouted loud and long, "To love and family!"

About the Author

"I spent all my life learning the rules. Now that I know which ones are irrelevant, life is simpler!"

AFTER MORE THAN thirty years as a busy family practice physician in Perth, Duncan Jefferson retired from his practice and started traveling. He still practices medicine part time, as a relief doctor traveling to the most remote corners of Australia, and in between assignments he and his wife travel the world.

Duncan has walked the famous Camino de Santiago, and now volunteers his time as the chairman of The Pilgrim

Trail Foundation, which is organizing a similar, contemplative-style walk in Australia called the Camino Salvado.

VISIT HIM ONLINE AT

WWW.DUNCANJEFFERSON.COM